Running Wild

HELEN GRIFFITHS

Running Wild

Illustrated by Victor Ambrus

HOLIDAY HOUSE · NEW YORK

For Sara

© Helen Griffiths 1977
Illustrations © Hutchinson Junior Books Ltd 1977
First American publication 1977 by Holiday House, Inc.
Printed in the United States of America

Library of Congress Cataloging in Publication Data

Griffiths, Helen.
  Running wild.

  SUMMARY: A young boy living with his grandparents
faces a dilemma when his dog has a second litter of
puppies that his grandparents cannot let him keep.
  [1. Dogs—Fiction] I. Ambrus, Victor G.
II. Title.
PZ7.G8837Rs3   [Fic]   77-3814
ISBN 0-8234-0309-2

I

Pablo lived with his grandparents on a small farm in Asturias. The farm was in a mountain valley where everything was emerald green except for the house, the colour of stone. By some standards, it could be considered a very poor house but it was like all the other houses and the only kind Pablo knew. It was small and cosy, with shuttered windows and a red-tiled roof. Big stones were piled on the roof because sometimes high winds or heavy snowfalls would make the tiles fall off. It was two-storeyed, and in the bottom part was the cowshed, with a little room next door with a stove, where the cooking and baking was done.

Pablo was eight years old. His hair was thick and dark and his eyes were brown. He was plump and round-faced because he drank plenty of fresh cow's milk, which his grandmother boiled first in a pot over the fire, and ate lots of new-laid eggs and home-made cheese. His grandparents loved him very dearly because he was their only grandson. They were inclined to spoil him and give him everything he asked for. He didn't ask for much; he really had everything he wanted except for one thing, and that was one need they couldn't satisfy.

He wanted to live with his parents. They had gone away when he was five to work in a country a long way away. His father hadn't wanted to stay on the farm, which wasn't really big enough to supply a livelihood for two families, but there was no work in the village, nor even in the nearest towns. So he had gone to Germany to work in a factory and, after a while, Pablo's mother had gone to join him. They both worked in the factory and sent money home to Pablo's grandparents to help them look after him and pay for the things he needed.

Pablo couldn't go with them though they couldn't really make him understand why. When he asked, his grandfather talked about laws and difficulties which made no sense to Pablo. He only knew that other children in the village lived with their parents, and he thought it very strange that in Germany it wasn't allowed. He had to stay behind with his grandparents and wait for his mother and father to come home. They sent him letters and toys and photos of themselves and said how much they loved and missed him. But they never said when they were coming home and this made Pablo sad sometimes.

It wasn't that he didn't love his grandparents. He loved them very much and was happy and contented most of the time. He helped his grandfather look after the ten cows, the several calves, the oxen and the pigs, and he helped his grandmother look after the chickens and the rabbits and the pigeons. He played with the baby rabbits, sometimes, when they were soft and smooth and almost as small as his hands. He watched the progress of the baby pigeons which came out of the eggs ugly and hairless and which looked uglier still, if that were possible, when spiky, speckled feathers first began to grow? And he would always be surprised when at last, he would see them smooth and handsome and perfectly feathered, emerging from the nest to care for themselves.

His grandmother liked to remind him of when he was smaller, about four or five, and she had shown him a pigeon's nest for the first time. He had looked at the pair of eggs, so much smaller than hen's eggs, and carefully listened while she explained that soon two baby pigeons would hatch from them. And then she had left him by himself because she had a lot of things to do.

Pablo had stayed, watching and watching, wondering how long it would take for the baby pigeons to appear. He wondered what they would look like inside the eggs, how there was even room for them, and in the end, tired of waiting – because Grandmother had said, 'Soon, very soon' – he got a stick and broke the shells himself, too impatient to wait any longer. He was very disappointed when two messy yolks ran through the twigs of the nest and wondered if his grandmother could be mistaken. Then he began to wonder if he might have done something wrong, so he threw the stick as far as he could and hurried away.

There was always plenty for him to watch and do and hardly ever any time for him to play with the tanks and

guns, trucks, and soldiers that his parents sent him from Germany. It was very exciting when his grandfather went down to the village post office to get the parcel with his name on it. Pablo would have liked to get it himself but the postman told him he had to be fourteen before he could sign the book for it, so Grandfather always had to collect it. It was no good Grandmother going because she couldn't write or sign her name.

Once Pablo dreamed that when he opened the parcel his parents were inside. Suddenly they were big and lifelike, hugging and kissing him, and saying how grown he was. But the dream very quickly disappeared because he didn't really know what they were like. The photos they sent were like pictures in the newspaper, strange, black and white faces that had nothing to do with him.

There was a school in the village, which looked very much like the neighbouring houses: small, with a red-tiled, mossy roof weighed down with stones, thick walls and green shutters over the windows. There was only one classroom and one teacher, who taught the six-year-olds their first letters and the fourteen-year-olds the rudiments of chemistry and physics, all in the same day. He was an energetic young man, full of enthusiasm, and the pupils appreciated him. He had come from the capital of the province and it was his first job, taking over when the last teacher had retired.

Pablo's parents sometimes sent postcards from Germany which the boy would take to school to show to the teacher. The teacher would show them to everyone so that they could see what that faraway city looked like and it made Pablo feel important, having his parents there and being the owner of the postcards that went round the classroom and were stuck on the wall. They were very dull postcards really. The one he liked best was the one they had sent him of an airplane.

'When are your parents coming home?' the teacher had once asked Pablo. His name was Don Elicio.

'When are my parents coming home?' Pablo asked his grandmother, more than once.

'One day. You'll see.'

The answer was always the same and Pablo hardly believed any more that the 'one day' would ever come and sometimes he was sad because he could no longer remember much about his mother and father, in spite of the letters and photos, and because the other boys talked about the things they did with their parents and he couldn't.

He was lonely, too. Most of the boys at school had brothers and sisters and they arrived in a crowd, running and colliding along the country lanes which led to the village, shouting challenges and jokes, sometimes fighting. But Pablo lived farther away than any of them and therefore went most of the way alone. Often as he took the path from his grandparents farm down to the village he could hear the other children's laughter and noise and the journey always seemed longer when he could hear their voices without being able to see them.

'Do you think they'll bring me a brother or sister when they come home?' he asked Grandmother.

'I doubt it,' she laughed. 'They'll have enough with you.'

'But I'd like one. We could do lots of things together.'

She chucked him under the chin. 'You can do lots of things with your grandfather.'

'I know but . . . Well, it's not the same.'

Grandmother didn't ask him what he meant because she already understood. She could see that he was sometimes lonely and wished that there was someone for him to play with. She saw how he played with the rabbits with a longing in his eyes; she saw how he watched the frisking calves with the same expression of need, and she wished there was some kind of companionship she could give him that would bring an end to his loneliness and his occasional sadness.

Above the cowshed of the little farmhouse were two bedrooms and a living room. A steep outdoor staircase led up to them. There wasn't a fireplace in the living room so that in winter, to keep warm, they all sat round a table whose thick green cloth reached the floor in heavy folds which could almost be wrapped round your waist and draped everybody's knees. Under the table, between the boards on which feet were perched, was a big round brazier which Grandmother prepared every afternoon with bits of charcoal whose ashes burned for hours. It was the cosiest thing Pablo knew. As yet his feet didn't reach the wooden board and the warmth crept up through the soles of his boots dangling above the ashes.

Grandmother would sit at the table and mend the clothes, Grandfather would write a letter to Germany, very slowly, with the writing paper placed over a piece of newspaper because he couldn't write over the tablecloth. Pablo would do his homework, or read a comic a boy at school might have given him. There was a big oil-lamp in the centre of the table which spread its yellowish light equally to all three of them, leaving the rest of the room to the furniture and its shadows, all in darkness.

Once in a letter Pablo's mother said that in Germany they didn't have braziers under the table. They had a thing called central heating which made everything so warm that you could walk around in your underwear if you wanted to, as if it were summer time. But Pablo, who sometimes liked to imagine that his mother was sitting in his grandmother's place, mending the clothes with the lamp's soft glow across her face, hoped she wouldn't bring the central heating back to the farm when at last she came home from Germany.

When it was time for bed, Grandmother would go down to the kitchen where water was simmering in a big black pot over the dying fire. She had a row of old cider bottles on a shelf which she filled with the hot water and stopped with a cork, and these they would take to bed with them to keep their feet warm until they fell asleep.

Every night Pablo prayed for his parents before he went to sleep and that winter he prayed for them to come home in time for Christmas. They had said they were going to send a special present because they had earned a lot of money that year, and Pablo thought the most special thing would be if

they bought a train ticket and came home to see him. The farmhouse was cosier at Christmas than at any other time, a sense of excitement and nostalgia adding to the warmth of the lamp and the brazier and the animals in their stalls below.

At Christmas time Grandmother brought the boxes out of the dresser which were Pablo's delight. In them, wrapped in cotton wool or tissue paper, were the different figures that went to make up the scene of Bethlehem which they constructed every year on the marble-topped chest in the living room.

Pablo painted a sheet of paper dark blue and then stuck on it stars cut out of the silver paper which Grandmother saved from chocolate bars. One star had to be bigger than all the rest, a comet with a streaming tail, and this was stuck in the centre, above the place where the stable would be set in which the Christ-child had been born.

He never tired of the different figures: the three Wise Men, one of them black-faced, with their camels; the shepherds with their flocks; the washerwoman, the knife-grinder, the wood-cutter, the ploughman with his team of oxen. They had been collected over the years. Some were made of wood, some of lead, and some were plastic – the newest ones – and it didn't matter that the wooden camels were taller than Herod's hill-top palace and the lead ploughman smaller than the plastic sheep. Each figure had its place and belonged there, whatever its size; the ducks on the pond, which was a little looking-glass from his mother's old handbag; the wood-cutter crossing the bridge over the river of silver paper; the Wise Men leading their camels up the hill to the lonely central stable where Mary, Joseph and the child Jesus clustered beneath the chocolate paper comet, their feet amid the bits of chopped-up straw which Pablo brought from their own stable underneath the living room.

They didn't have a Christmas tree, although the forest was full of pines which were thinned out each year and sent to the cities for people to buy and decorate. Pablo's mother said that in Germany everybody had a Christmas tree but in the Spanish farmhouse, with Christmas trees growing all around, no one had heard of such a custom until recently.

This year, when Pablo set out the little cork houses and the figures with such care, he was sure his parents would be there to see them. He set the Christ-child in the cradle, close to the kneeling Virgin's side, and wondered what it would be like to have a baby brother in a cot beside his bed. Perhaps they would come, and the special present would be a baby brother, so that even if they had to go away again they'd leave him someone to play with. Only a few days earlier, a boy at school had told him that the doctor had brought his mother a baby girl from Paris, which was in France. If babies could come from France so unexpectedly, surely they could come from Germany too?

With one finger he carefully pushed the donkey and the oxen closer to the holy family, wondering as he did so if that stable had been like his own home in winter, with the cows underneath, rustling and stamping, giving out their special warm smell. But the baby Jesus was luckier than he because His mother and father were right beside him. They hadn't left Him behind when they went away, not even when King Herod was chasing them.

He sighed. If only they would come back that Christmas, he would be the happiest boy alive.

2

On the crests of the highest mountains there was always snow, even in summertime. Pablo could see the snow from his grandparents' farm. It glinted in the sunlight and looked like silver. On the lower slopes the snow melted and trickled into the streams which had gouged a way through the hills and forests to become great rushing rivers in the valleys long before the first men had ever seen them. The water in the streams was always ice-cold, even on the hottest summer day. Because there was so much water, from the snow as well as the rain, trees grew thick and dark all about the mountains. Only the crests were bare because it was too cold up there for grass or trees; there wasn't any earth, just rocks and pebbles below the snow line.

Dark, heavy pine trees and immense, lighter-coloured oaks and chestnuts fringed Grandfather's land. In some of the fields baby pine trees were springing up from the seeds which had fallen and taken root in the good black earth. Some were smaller than Pablo. Others were about the same size.

'And about the same age, I expect,' said his grandfather. 'They take a long time to grow.'

Pablo stretched his head back as far as it would go to look at the tops of some of the giant trees. If you climbed to the very highest branches he was sure you could touch the sky.

'How old can they be then?' he wondered.

'Perhaps two hundred years. Perhaps more. These forests are thousands of years old.'

Pablo felt there must be something magic in the forest where the trees were so ancient and gigantic. His grandfather

liked to go into the forest to hunt, and sometimes he too
Pablo with him, with his brown and white hunting dog.

'You must never go into the forest alone,' he told the boy.
'It can be dangerous.'

'Why is it dangerous?' He wondered if the trees, being so
old, might fall down on him.

'There are a lot of wild animals in the forest, that's why.
Bears and wolves and wild cats.'

'I've never seen any,' argued Pablo. He had only ever
seen rabbits and squirrels with any frequency and a glimpse
so doubtful of deer among the bracken and bushes that he
could hardly believe he had seen them.

'Take my word for it then. I've heard the cats screaming and I've seen my share of wild pigs.'

'But the bears,' insisted Pablo. 'Have you ever seen a bear?'

Grandfather admitted that he hadn't. 'But other men have. Sometimes they come down to the farms and kill the cattle.'

'Has that ever happened to our cattle?'

'No, but I've heard of it happening elsewhere. And one year a bear went into the village and nearly frightened all the people to death.'

'What! Our village?'

'Another one, but it might have been ours.'

Pablo was sometimes tempted to enter the forest alone but once he got beyond the fringes there were places where the sunlight suddenly vanished. It became dark and silent, with glimpses of light few and far between. He would feel goose pimples on his arms and shivers down his spine, and he was glad to rush out to the fields again where the sun was bright and there were no shadows in which bears and wolves could linger.

He asked Don Elicio about bears because he didn't always believe everything Grandfather told him. Grandfather told tall stories sometimes, which once he had always believed, but now that he was eight he preferred to find things out for himself. At school he learned things that his grandfather didn't know and this sometimes made him feel uncomfortable. He wanted Grandfather to be cleverer than he was and this was another reason for wanting his father to come home. He was sure that his father, like Don Elicio, must know everything.

'Oh yes,' said the teacher, 'there are bears in the forest. Not many because people have been killing them for so long that they've almost been exterminated.'

'What's that?' asked Pablo. 'Extermi–, ex– what you said?'

'Wiped out. Destroyed.'

'And why do people kill them?'

'They say it's because they spoil the crops and kill the animals but more often it's because men feel brave and clever if they kill one. Bears sleep all through the winter and when they wake up in the spring they're very hungry. That's when they're most likely to maraud about the farms, when the fish aren't yet jumping in the rivers and there aren't enough berries on the trees.'

Don Elicio talked a lot about bears and Pablo learned how they ate and ate throughout the summer so that when winter came they would be rolling with fat that must last them the long winter through. He learned that the cubs were born in the wintertime and that when at last they came out of their dens the father bears would eat them if they could. He drew a picture of a father bear trying to eat its cub but Grandmother didn't like it and wouldn't send it to Germany in the next letter.

Pablo's parents didn't return that Christmas and the special surprise they had prepared for him finally destroyed his wavering belief that the presents he found in the living room every sixth of January had been brought by the three Kings. His grandparents, almost children themselves in some things, had fostered his belief, delighting in it, bolstering it even when he came home from school with doubts.

That Christmas his father sent a money order from Germany and a letter, telling Grandfather to take Pablo to the nearest town to buy him a bike. It was such a lot of money to be spent on a small boy that, at first, they had their doubts about it. Wouldn't it be better to save it for the future? Would a bike even be much use in the stony lanes? But Pablo imagined himself on the bike. He hadn't seen any other boy in the village with one – not even the biggest boys – so in the end Grandfather gave in with a sigh saying that, after all, the money had been sent for that purpose.

A few days after Christmas they went on the bus to buy the bike. It had been snowing and the plough had been up and down the main road earlier that day, piling up the snow in drifts on either side in grey-splattered chunks. Pablo looked through the misted windows, seeing only hedges and trees and old stone walls amid the whiteness, trying to imagine what having a bike would be like. The postman had one, black with big wheels, but no one else.

On the way back in the same bus, a few hours later, the bike was tied to the roof among the bundles and baskets. It shone in the sun that was melting holes through the snow in the fields. All the children were at the bus-stop, awaiting the bike's arrival, and a dozen pairs of hands reached up for it when the driver handed it down. Pablo felt very important and pleased with himself, and so did Grandfather.

Everyone asked for a ride and Pablo was glad Grandfather was there to say no, because he wouldn't have had the courage to and he wanted to be the first to mount it. He didn't know how to ride it so he wheeled the bike up the lanes, hardtrodden with snow, and the audience followed, dropping back bit by bit as they drew farther and farther away from the village. Hands smoothed the black leather saddle, fingers touched the shiny handlebars; someone bolder than the rest dared to press the bell, startling them all.

'Off with you, off with you!' cried Grandfather. 'There'll be plenty of time for you all to ride it, but no one's touching it before my grandson.'

He waved his arms and shooed them off and soon the two of them were alone, plodding homewards up the hill.

The spokes were splashed with mud by the time the farmyard was reached and the sun had gone so that the bike didn't seem so shiny, but Grandmother came out of her kitchen wiping her hands on her apron, mouth open with admiration. She ruffled Pablo's head and said, 'What a lucky grandson I have. You're being treated very well this year!'

Pablo spent what was left of the daylight learning to ride the red bike. He fell off countless times, grazing his cheek and knuckles, tearing his trousers, but by the time he wearily climbed the stairs to the living room, having scrubbed off the mud and blood in the yard, he could ride it as well as the postman.

The next day he took it down to the village, jarring every bone in his body as the wheels bounced over the stones. He filled his pockets with marbles, chewing gum and packets of sunflower seeds in exchange for turns on the bike, and that day at least he was the most popular boy in the village. Even the twelve-year-olds condescended to talk to him.

But on the sixth day of January, when he dashed bright-eyed to the living room straight from his bed to see what the three Kings had left him overnight, there was nothing but a box of coloured pencils and a pair of strong black boots.

He couldn't believe it. Surely he hadn't been so bad that year! Other years he'd been naughtier and they'd left him more things. Last year there'd been . . . He racked his memory. Well, lots of things. He couldn't exactly remember. The box of games . . . the robot that worked with batteries . . . lots more than this.

Grandmother shuffled into the room. She was wearing her old dressing gown, which looked like an eiderdown with its thick, stuffed squares, and carried a tray with a big mug of cocoa and a plateful of biscuits. He looked at her, managing to blink the involuntary tear of disappointment away, but not before she had seen it.

'What's the matter, Pablo? Don't you feel well?'

'The Kings. They've hardly left me anything. Why? Why? I don't think I've been so very bad.'

'And the bike?' she reminded him, placing the tray on the table. 'What about that, or have you forgotten it already?' Her tone was sharp.

'But that was a present from my parents.'

'And where do you suppose all the other presents have come from then? You've never had so much as this year and on top of that you complain.'

Now Grandmother wasn't in a good mood that morning. Overnight an animal had stolen into the hen run and killed a dozen birds. She had found their bedraggled bodies scattered on every side, torn or half eaten, not even fit for their own consumption. She'd had a row with her husband because for the last three months he'd been promising to get a new dog to replace the one that had died, and to hear Pablo complaining with tears in his eyes was just too much for her. As much as she had delighted only a year earlier in telling him how the Kings had come to see her to ask what Pablo wanted, describing each one in detail with their cloaks of gold and silver, their silk turbans of many colours, she just as abruptly told him that he should consider himself about the luckiest boy in the village and that he didn't deserve to have parents who threw money away on such senseless things when twelve of her chickens lay dead in the yard.

What with his first disappointment, Grandmother's bad temper and the fact that he'd fallen asleep the night before convinced that, with the magic of which only the Kings were capable, his parents would be brought from Germany and would be sitting in the living room with huge smiles and open arms, Pablo's morning was ruined. He didn't feel hungry and played about with the cocoa and biscuits until Grandmother impatiently snatched the tray away and sent him to get dressed. He hadn't even bothered to pick up the pencils or try on the boots and when he got downstairs and saw Grandfather throwing the dead chickens into a sack, he decided to keep out of his way, too.

He pulled his bike out of the barn. It was no longer bright and had the muck of the yard stuck to its wheels and mudguards. He pedalled away but as soon as the farm was out of sight he stopped. He didn't know where to go or what to do. The lanes were thick with snow and riding the bike was hard work. It was easier to walk, assuming you wanted to get somewhere. His toes were beginning to feel the cold, so he stamped his feet up and down, blowing on his fingers at the same time. He'd forgotten to wear his gloves and scarf and now even his ears were feeling the bite of the bleak air. His heart felt as bleak as the countryside and his thoughts were as dark as the forest.

It wasn't true about the Kings. It never had been true but they had made him believe it. Perhaps it wasn't true about his parents, either, that one day they'd return. Perhaps really they didn't want him any more and would never come, and if they had any more children they would have them in Germany and forget all about him because they didn't need him.

Pain – a mixture of anger and despair – seethed inside him. In the village all the children were indoors with their parents. Perhaps they didn't have a bike but who wanted a bike anyway? You couldn't really use it. It was a nuisance more often than not, just like now. It was hard work pushing it through the snow. And that was the special surprise! He'd already forgotten the excitement of going to town to buy it, the pride that had swelled his heart when everyone wanted to touch it and ride it. It was just a bit of hard, cold metal, spreadeagled over the snow. It wasn't even new any more.

He knew that in a way his grandparents disapproved of it. Although they didn't say so, they too thought it was time his parents came home. Instead of sending the money for a bike, if they had so much to spare why didn't they come home?

With a cry of angry misery, he gave the bike a kick, sending up a spray of snow with his boot. The machine registered no feeling at all, not even a shiver.

3

Grandmother's hens were not the only victims of the night's marauder. When Grandfather walked down to the village later that morning to have his usual glass of Sunday cider (it wasn't Sunday but as it was a holiday it was just the same) he heard another farmer complaining, too. This man had a few bullocks in a sheltered field not far from the village. They had an open shed in which to sleep and for this reason he didn't shut them in his barn at night, not having enough room for them. When he went to take them some fodder that morning he found three of them weak from loss of blood which still trickled from terrible wounds in their haunches and bellies.

'It must be wolves,' he was saying. 'There are prints all over the field.'

'Wolves?' queried a younger man sceptically. He had never seen a wolf. It was only the old men who talked about wolves. 'Surely they wouldn't come so near the village?'

'If they were hungry enough they would.'

Grandfather went with the farmer and all the rest to inspect the bullocks. The vet went with them. He tended the injured animals as best he could before declaring it would be better to slaughter them. He said they had been attacked by dogs or wolves. The jumbled prints all over the field confirmed his opinion.

'We've got wolves then, after all these years!' someone exclaimed.

'Could be,' but the vet scratched his head doubtfully. 'Could be,' he said again, 'but I'm more inclined to think of dogs. There's been no wolves about these parts for so long.'

Then all the village dogs came under suspicion. They were inspected one by one but none carried any telltale blood marks. Most of them were kept tied up, anyway.

Grandfather brought the men back to his own farm, the vet among them. They examined what prints they could find but, as there had been a snowfall overnight, no one could tell where they led to. Grandmother was among them, scolding her husband, reminding him he should have got another dog when the other died.

'If we'd had a dog this wouldn't have happened. It would have frightened the wolf away. All these years we've kept a dog and we've never had trouble before.'

'Right, right,' he answered her, trying to soothe her. 'We'll get another dog.'

'A fine time to do it,' she snorted, 'now that the hens are dead. My best layers, too.'

Pablo hung about near the men. They were all talking at once and no one took much notice of Grandmother who didn't take much notice of them either. Eventually they all went away, still arguing, after having decided to get out their dogs that afternoon and hunt through the forest for what they might find.

'Can I come too?' Pablo begged his grandfather.

The excitement had made him forget his earlier misery, and his imagination was fired with the talk he had overheard. He had forgotten it was the day of the Kings and didn't even take much notice of the special meal Grandmother had prepared, roast suckling pig and potatoes, with apples baked in their jackets for afterwards.

He wore his thickest jersey under his coat and Grandmother tied a scarf round his ears, telling her husband to make sure he didn't remove it. The afternoon sky was lead-coloured, laden with snow. Grandfather glanced up at it wryly.

'We're not going to see much in the forest,' he remarked as he went to let his gun dog out of the barn.

Grandmother had come to see them off. 'If that animal

was any good,' she said, crossly shooing off its exuberant greetings, 'it would have barked.'

'Perhaps it did and we didn't hear it.'

'Hmm. A mastiff's the thing for keeping wolves away. My father always used to have one, and we never lost any of the stock to wolves.'

'All right, woman. Tomorrow I'll go down to the village and see if I can get one,' he promised, and he put his arm round Pablo's shoulders as they marched off, the gun dog cavorting over the snow, kicking it up with its clumsy paws. 'Your grandmother's a good woman,' he told him confidentially, 'but sometimes she nags too much. All women are the same.'

Pablo grinned. He knew what his grandfather meant and felt very warmly towards him that afternoon. He had forgotten that he had wanted his own father to come back for Christmas and stretched his legs as far as he could to keep up with the other's pace.

A dozen men tramped through the forest that dark afternoon with twice as many dogs either in front or behind them. They shot a couple of rabbits and half a dozen wood pigeons but neither the gun dogs nor the mastiffs showed any signs of scenting bigger game, not even deer.

'But a wolf can travel a hundred kilometres in a night,' one of them said, 'and he's not likely to do his hunting on his own doorstep. We're just wasting our time.'

There was no doubt that the mysterious predator or predators had completely vanished without trace. Pablo was disappointed. His head was filled with the old stories of wolves, their cunning, their wickedness, their cruelty, and his heart had beat fast with excitement at the thought of meeting one face to face. One of the men had talked about shooting them right between the eyes, others had made wild guesses as to their size, and they all had some tale or another to tell. If only he could actually see one, even if it was dead! But all he saw were the rabbits and the pigeons and he felt a bit sorry for the rabbits, whose eyes bulged sightlessly as they hung from the hunter's belt.

Soon it was too dark to see anything and the men tramped back across the fields, stopping at Grandfather's farm for a glass of cider from the barrel he kept in the barn. The cider came from his own apples in the orchard behind the house. It had a better taste than the stuff they sold in bottles, Grandmother always said, and no one disagreed.

'I knew you wouldn't find anything,' Grandmother greeted them all, but she was in a good mood now because it wasn't often that so many people crowded into her living room, and it was a special day after all. Some of the men were friends of her son and it gave her an excuse to talk about him.

She cut big chunks from one of the smoked hams hanging in the kitchen chimney and let Pablo carve up the big round loaf with Grandfather's knife. She wanted everyone to see how clever he was. Normally she wouldn't let him touch the knife because it was far too sharp for him.

Pablo stuffed himself with ham and bread and cider, his cheeks burning red from the icy forest, the warm room and the drink. Soon he seemed to be floating and all he could remember of that winter night was the deep strong sound of men's voices and laughter, the glowing lamp and a warm, deep sense of belonging. Afterwards he thought it was the very best day he had ever known.

When he woke up the next morning his head ached terribly. Grandmother told him to stay in bed and brought him some cocoa and biscuits. It was very dark in the room although it was late and Grandmother told him that there would be a tremendous snowfall very soon.

'Where's Grandfather?' he asked.

'He's gone down to the village to see if he can bring back a dog. I'm not losing any more hens if I can help it.'

'Why didn't he take me with him?'

'He was going to but you were still snoring when he'd finished with the cows.' She pinched his chin. 'You drank far too much cider yesterday, my lad. I didn't notice with all the to do. Your father did the same once, only he went and fell down the stairs. Lucky he didn't hurt himself.'

'Has the wolf been again?' he wanted to know.

'Not that I know of. Now finish up your breakfast. I've got work to do.'

She left him on his own and he cuddled back under the eiderdown. He didn't feel very well, and it was so dark that it was more like night-time instead of morning. He must have fallen asleep for all of a sudden he heard his grandfather shouting, 'Where's the lad got to? I've something to show him.'

Pablo heard his footsteps crossing the living room and a moment later he was beside the bed, pushing something towards him as he struggled out of his dreams.

'Look what I've got for you. See if you like it. Your grandmother says it's good for nothing but I know you won't think the same.'

He thrust a warm little body into his arms and Pablo found himself staring down at the tiniest puppy he had ever seen, all wrinkles and paws and thick grey fur.

'It hasn't got any eyes!' he cried, alarmed.

'Of course it has,' Grandfather laughed, 'but it hasn't opened them yet. It was born only three days ago.'

Grandmother had followed him into the room.

'I sent you for a dog and you come back with that thing! How do you suppose that's going to keep the wolves away?'

'It'll grow, woman. It'll grow.'

'And a bitch, too. What's the use of that?'

'But you like it, don't you, Pablo? Do you want me to take it back? The man was going to drown them all and the mother was a good-looking dog, half mastiff, as big as a calf. It'll grow, never you fear.'

'Well, I can't see you chaining that thing out to the kennel. It'll get lost in the straw, and I'm not looking after it.'

'That'll be Pablo's job, won't it,' he said, giving the boy a wink, and Pablo grinned back at him, hardly able to believe his good fortune.

4

The days were too dark and snowy for Pablo to be able to return to school when the new term started. At any other time this could have upset him because he enjoyed playing with the boys, exchanging news with them and listening to Don Elicio, but with the puppy in his possession, needing so much care and attention, he completely forgot about everything else.

The first morning, when Grandmother had stopped grumbling, she went to heat up some milk for it, diluting it with water because cow's milk was far too rich and strong for such a small creature. She came upstairs with a bowl in her hands and an old rag for Pablo to put over his knees while he fed her to save his clothes from spills, but after ten minutes both puppy and boy were utterly frustrated and half the milk was on the floor or soaking the cloth.

The puppy only knew how to suck and was hardly able to do even this with much skill. Pablo, after first sticking the bowl under her nose and expecting her to drink, tried giving it to her with his fingers. Perhaps his fingers were too small, or the milk they scooped up insufficient for her ravening appetite, or perhaps she didn't recognize the taste. Whatever it was, the puppy cried and struggled and Pablo grew cross, and they both got very sticky and damp.

After watching all this, Grandmother took over. She dipped her puppy's muzzle right into the bowl, causing her to splutter and choke and scrabble frantically. Then she tried putting milk round her mouth for her to lick, but the puppy didn't know how to lick and only got wetter and stickier still. Grandmother had more patience than Pablo, because more than once she had reared an orphaned animal, but she had never tried to feed a three-day-old puppy before and sighed helplessly.

'She'll die. She'll die!' cried Pablo anxiously. 'Let me try again, Grandmother. Let me try again.'

He cradled the tiny, woolly animal in his arms, trying to calm her, upset by her whimperings and occasional burst of high-pitched howls, while Grandmother held the bowl, already half empty and its contents almost cold. The black wool round the puppy's muzzle was all sticky and Pablo tried to wipe it dry with the rag – a vain effort because the rag was just about as wet and sticky as the puppy.

Somehow the little animal caught the rag in her mouth and again began to suck frantically, with such strength that when Pablo tried to pull it out he couldn't. Grandmother cut short his exclamation and held his arm.

'Let her, let her. Look,' she said, and she dipped what she could of the rag into the bowl. Some milk was soaked up by it and the puppy went on sucking.

'Do you think she's getting anything?' asked Pablo excitedly. 'Grandmother, do you think she's getting anything?'

'Something at least. It'll keep her quiet for a while till we think of something better. Perhaps a teaspoon . . . '

She put the bowl in his hand. 'You go on with her as she is while I bring a teaspoon and some more milk. This is so cold and dirty now.'

While Grandmother was gone Pablo discovered that the puppy was happier if he put a couple of fingers inside the rag. Like that she sucked better. He felt the tremendous pull on his fingers and smiled to himself. How strong she was and yet how small!

Grandmother came back with another breakfast bowl and a teaspoon. 'You hold her,' she said, 'while I try spooning it into her mouth.'

This attempt was about as successful as the rest. Most of the milk slid out of the anxious jaws. Very little of it actually reached her hungry stomach but at last the puppy was still, either satisfied or worn out with trying.

'It's going to be hard work rearing her, Pablo,' warned his grandmother. 'Especially at this cold time. Baby animals need lots of warmth. They snuggle up to their mothers who feed them and lick them clean. She hasn't got a mother now so you're going to have to be like a mother to her.'

Pablo nodded happily, hardly tearing his gaze away from the sleeping grey form to glance at his grandmother.

'Isn't she pretty?' he said.

Grandmother nodded. 'But did you hear what I said?' she asked him. 'I haven't got time to be helping you with her and as soon as the weather clears you must go back to school. Then who's going to bother with her?'

'You'll help me. It'll only be for a little while when I'm at school. As soon as I come home I'll look after her.'

'And what about your homework? You'll start forgetting it to play with the puppy.'

'No, I won't. I promise I won't. I'll do my homework and look after her and she won't be any trouble at all.'

Grandmother nodded wryly, knowing very well that Pablo's promises were heartfelt but not likely to be kept. Hadn't he wanted to look after the rabbits and after three days tired of taking them food and fresh water? Hadn't he once begged to give an orphaned calf its bottle and then complained how his arms ached after only two minutes?

'We'll see, we'll see,' she answered. 'But remember one thing. If you don't look after it, it'll surely die. It's only very, very tiny.'

She went away with the dirty bowls and the soggy rag, leaving Pablo in contemplation of the puppy sleeping in his arms.

He looked at the thick, thick fur, all grey except for the black muzzle and a shadow of blackness about the deeply furrowed skull. The little ears were completely flattened against her head. They pointed upwards and seemed to be made of rubber. The head was so blunt and wrinkled that it was hardly possible to distinguish the closed eye slits except by the slightly darker line which ran from corners to cheek.

She half rolled over as he changed the position of his arm, which was feeling her weight, and to his surprise he saw that, in spite of the thick wool all over her, her underside was completely bare. He carefully ran a finger over the grey skin. The place where the cord had been was not quite healed. It was exactly in the middle of her stomach and she had five black teats in a row on either side, hardly bigger than pin-heads. He grinned as he counted them, thinking as he did so, 'She'll be able to have ten puppies one day. Ten!'

Then he saw her claws, tiny, soft and black, and the little black pads, as soft as the skin on her stomach. He had never examined anything so closely as he examined that puppy and yet it seemed that the more he looked at her the more he found something to marvel. Her head was very big compared to the rest of her body, while the hindquarters seemed the smallest of all. Her paws were also huge. In fact there was more head and paws than anything else, and a slim little tail at the end, almost stuck to her body, with a black stripe that started at the tail tip and went all the way up to the shoulders.

He couldn't imagine her ever being big enough to fight off wolves or guard the house from intruders and, even as he thought this, he knew he didn't want Grandfather ever to chain her up to the stone kennel in front of the house. She wouldn't be his then. She wouldn't really belong to him.

He began to think of the old dog that had died and found he could hardly remember what it had looked like. It wasn't like having a dog when it was chained up night and day. He vaguely recalled that it had been big and shaggy and he suddenly remembered the expression of weary resignation in its eyes – it had never meant anything to him before, that expression, not until he tried to imagine this warm little thing chained up there in its place – and it suddenly came to him in a flash the awfulness of spending a whole lifetime in the same place, condemned to eternal imprisonment without hope of reprieve.

He remembered his grandfather sighing, 'Poor old thing,'

when he found it frozen with its head between its paws one morning. They hadn't even noticed when it was dead at first because so often it had lain there with its head between its paws, and then it was gone and Pablo hadn't even wondered until now what had happened to it.

A coldness passed through his heart as he thought of this little thing ending the same way and he wondered why Grandfather had treated his guard dog and his hunting dog with such difference. It was true that the hunting dog was also chained up, in the barn, but whenever Grandfather went hunting or for a walk through the fields and forest the dog went with him, dashing about like a mad thing, yellow eyes sparkling with delight.

When he asked Grandfather about this difference at dinner, the old man answered, 'Well, you see, a hunting dog is for hunting and a guard dog is for guarding.'

It wasn't a very satisfactory answer for Pablo, worrying about his puppy's future but not even daring to express his anxiety in the hope that they might forget they had brought the puppy to the farm for guarding.

'But don't guard dogs like to run about too? Do they like being chained up all the time?'

'What questions the boy asks!' exclaimed Grandmother with amusement as she ladled a thick potato soup into his plate.

Grandfather pondered for a while. The truth was that it was not a matter he had thought about. As long as he could remember mastiffs had always been chained somewhere in front of the house or near the hen-runs and hunting dogs had always been kept in the barn. He did as his father and grandfather had done. In the end he said, 'It's a question of duty. You know what duty is?'

Pablo nodded. It wasn't one of his favourite words and it had a disagreeable tone about it.

'That's it. Duty,' repeated Grandfather, satisfied with his answer. 'Duty has nothing to do with likes or dislikes. It's just something you do because you have to.'

Pablo sighed and said no more. His glance wandered to

the wooden box against the wall where the puppy was sleeping, curled up in a sack from the barn with some straw underneath, and he wondered what duty was awaiting her when one day she was strong and 'as big as a calf' as Grandfather insisted she was going to be.

'And now it's your duty to eat up that soup before it gets cold,' Grandmother broke into his thoughts, seeing where his gaze had strayed. 'I knew how it would be,' she began to grumble. 'With that puppy in the house you don't do anything but daydream over her. You should be looking at your school books. Heaven knows how much you're missing. When will this weather change!'

Never, hoped Pablo deep inside himself. Bound to the farm, almost completely bound to the house with its warmth and gentle lamp-glow, he felt as safe as a silkworm inside its cocoon. It was too cold for the puppy to be sent to the barn, even too cold to leave it in the kitchen. Everything went on in the one big living room: Grandmother peeling potatoes, Grandfather sharpening his tools, the puppy sleeping and himself pretending to study when they insisted but with the puppy always nearby.

School was a long way off. There was only now and the happiness of now. Tomorrow and duty were as vague as the shadows in the corners of the room.

5

More than a fortnight went by before Pablo was able to return to school, and in that short time the puppy had done a lot of growing. She was still very much a baby, sleeping most of the time, but she had doubled in size and was able to lap milk from a bowl without too much difficulty. Pablo had to feed her about six times a day. At first she cried in the night for food, too, but it was far too cold to get out of bed. Grandmother wouldn't let him and neither would she get out of bed herself, so soon the puppy learned she must sleep while it was dark and not expect to be fed.

Except for her colour, she looked very much like a bear cub, Pablo thought, with her big blunt head, huge paws and round, round body. She drank a lot of milk and always seemed hungry. By the time Pablo was going back to school, Grandmother had suggested he should start putting some cereal in her milk to make it more filling.

She was so heavy on her legs that she could hardly walk, in spite of her efforts to do so. At first she moved backwards, pushing with her front legs and sliding along on her bottom, which made Pablo laugh out loud. Whenever she tried to move forwards, she fell over. But she never gave up trying and, with wagging tail and shaking head, would stumble and trip and slide about the living room, each day growing stronger and more self-confident.

Pablo had to write a letter to his parents to thank them for the bike and tell them about the recent festivities. He did all this in the first two sentences and then wrote another two pages all about the puppy, adding a drawing of her at the end on the third page. Grandfather read the letter out loud before putting it in the envelope, looking for spelling mistakes and to make sure the handwriting was good. He was very proud of Pablo's handwriting, which was much clearer than his own, and wanted his parents to know that even though they weren't there to watch over him, his grandparents were.

Grandmother said he shouldn't have written so much about the puppy. 'You should have told them about other things, too.'

'What other things?' asked Pablo with surprise. For him there were no other things, only that chunky warm creature into whose fur coat he plunged his face each morning as soon as he got up.

By the time she was five weeks old she was pretty steady on her legs and was tired of milk and cereals. She wolfed down the mashed-up leftovers that Pablo gave her and gnawed at a knuckle-bone which he put in her box. She wagged her tail, her eyes sparkling, her whole body wriggling with joy whenever she woke up and found Pablo near her and followed him wherever he went, more than once getting under his feet and tripping him up.

'That puppy will have to go downstairs,' Grandmother warned. 'She's getting too big to be up here.'

'But she's still only a baby,' pleaded Pablo. 'Let her stay up here. I won't hear her when she cries if she's downstairs.'

'And what's she going to cry for? Besides, the house is no

place for an animal. Look at the messes she makes on the floor!'

Pablo didn't know how to defend the puppy. It was true that she was dirty, but only because she didn't know it was wrong. But he was afraid of her being banned from the house, feeling sure that it was a step nearer to her being chained to the kennel.

There had been no more signs of the marauding animal which had done so much damage at Christmas, but other villages had been attacked. In one two ponies had been killed, in another dozens of chickens, while in a third a farmer said he had actually seen a big, reddish-grey wolf trotting calmly along between the houses just after dawn. He had run home for his rifle but by the time he was back in the street the animal had disappeared.

After talking over these events at home, Grandfather had said, 'Well, we'll be safe enough once that puppy of yours grows, won't we, my lad?'

Pablo had nodded, forcing a smile, but a shadow fell over him at the words. He would have begged Grandfather not to chain the dog up when she was bigger but was afraid to speak, just in case Grandfather hadn't thought about it and was given the idea by his words. Thinking it over Grandfather hadn't ever actually said the puppy was to be a guard dog, although he had gone to the village to look for one. Perhaps it was a present from the Kings.

He tried to remember Grandfather's actual words when he had handed him the puppy, but couldn't. He had been half asleep and the moment had been so exciting that all he recalled was the feel of her in his arms. Had he said the puppy was for him? If that were so, then he couldn't really oblige him to chain her up one day. Then again, since the puppy had been brought home and in spite of Grandmother scornfully saying that she would be useless for guarding, there had been no more talk of replacing the old dog, which could mean that they did indeed intend to take her away from him one day.

This constant fear overshadowed all his days with her,

especially now that she was leaving babyhood behind and could romp and play and even utter sharp, high-pitched barks, sounds of excitement and joy. She was growing so big and strong and lively that, just as Grandmother had already said she must leave the house, Grandfather would one day realize that she was big enough to start learning her duty.

Every morning when he set out for school, tramping down the snowy lanes with his satchel on his back, he would be gripped with worry. Would he find her chained up when he came back home?

The chain became a symbol. Once it was round her neck it would never be undone. It haunted him constantly, especially because he could never talk about it, not daring to remind his grandfather of it, rusting amid the slush and rotting straw, unmoved since it had been taken from the dead dog's neck and thrown there. He even went to stare at it. It was something odious and unrelenting, unfeeling, uncaring. It would make a prisoner of his lovely puppy, and her days of jumping and crawling all over him would be gone forever. He hated that chain. He wanted to stamp on it and crush it, but it frightened him so much that he dared not even touch it.

One night he dreamed about it. He dreamed that it was round his neck, heavy, terribly heavy. He was only very little and at first it was far too big. Then, bit by bit, he began to grow, get fatter. But the chain stayed the same, heavy, hot, rusting into his neck, growing tighter and tighter, so tight that when he tried to call for help his voice was strangled. His throat felt that it would burst in the chain's grip until at last, in utter desperation, a scream burst from him.

In a second he was awake. Grandmother was there, in her long white nightdress with a black shawl thrown over her shoulders, peering anxiously at him in the light of the oil lamp, soothingly repeating his name. He felt her bony fingers on his forehead which burned with his fear.

'The chain, the chain,' he whispered. He could hardly

talk, his throat hurt so much, and he put his hands up to his neck, knowing now it was only a dream but still inwardly gripped with fear.

'You've been dreaming,' she soothed him. 'It was only a bad dream,' but even as she rested her hand on his forehead and then his wrist, she shook her head and tutted worriedly. 'You're burning,' she told him.

'My throat hurts,' he croaked. 'It was the chain. . . .'

'We'll have to call the doctor tomorrow. You've probably got tonsillitis. I'll give you an aspirin now. That'll help to get your temperature down.'

She hadn't understood about the chain and, as Pablo came out of his dream and realized what she was saying, he was suddenly content. If he had tonsillitis he wouldn't be able to go to school. He would be able to stay with the puppy and Grandfather wouldn't be able to chain her up without his knowledge.

He stayed at home for a week. Grandmother didn't want him in the kitchen, where he could catch a chill, so the puppy was allowed to stay upstairs, too. She was too big for the box now and slept on a sack and an old bit of horse blanket that Grandfather had found in the barn. Her appetite was ravenous and, although her teeth were still not strong enough to do much chewing, she managed to swallow everything that was put down for her, as well as two big bowls of milk both night and morning.

Grandfather laughed at her appetite, remarking, 'That dog's too well fed. She's going to be a giant and the handsomest dog in the district if Pablo has any say in the matter.'

'As soon as you're better she's going downstairs,' Grandmother said to Pablo. 'I've had enough of the mess she makes up here. And she's big enough now not to catch cold.'

'What are you going to call her?' said Grandfather.

Pablo stared at him thoughtfully. For all that he loved her, for all that she filled all his waking thoughts and most of his dreams, he hadn't given her a name. The dog in the yard hadn't had a name and neither had the hunting dog, who answered to a whistle or a shout. He called her 'beautiful' most of the time but that wasn't a proper name for a dog.

'What can I call her?' he asked.

Grandfather said, 'My father used to have a dog like her. A beauty she was. Big, like a donkey. And fierce. She killed three wolves in her lifetime. Tore them to pieces.'

Grandmother interrupted with a scornful grunt. 'With the way this boy spoils her, she'll grow up a soft good-for-nothing. All she'll be able to tear to pieces are my rugs and table-cloths. He's making a real softy of her. It's time she started to learn she's a dog.'

Grandfather burst out laughing. 'I do believe she thinks she's a human being. She's sharp all right.'

Pablo's heart had clenched with dread at Grandmother's words. Suddenly all his half-forgotten fears returned. He must speak up now or it would be too late. Grandmother noticed his sudden blenching and looked alarmed.

'What's the matter, Pablo? Do you feel worse? Does your throat hurt again?'

He shook his head fiercely and, taking a deep breath which made his shoulders and chest heave noticeably, frightening Grandmother still more, he blurted, 'Grandfather, promise me you'll never chain her up like the old dog. Promise me you'll never chain her up. Please. Please. Promise me.'

So intense was his gaze, so dark his eyes and pale his face, they immediately realized that this was a fear that had long tormented him. And Grandmother suddenly remembered his half-gasped words, 'the chain, the chain', that had made no sense to her then.

'But, Pablo, you know your grandfather brought her to replace the old dog and – '

'But she doesn't have to be chained. She can fight wolves far better if she's not chained and, and – well, I don't want her to be chained.'

Sobs stopped him from saying any more. They were sobs of relief more than anything else, because at last his fear was out.

'You surely don't think she's going to stay up here all the time,' began Grandmother again.

'No, but – please.'

He looked from one to the other and they caught his gaze and looked at each other too. Neither of them quite knew what the other was thinking. Both wanted to make Pablo happy. They both started to speak at the same time.

'She can sleep in the barn, I suppose . . . ' began Grandfather.

'Perhaps we can find her a corner in the kitchen,' were Grandmother's first words.

'But what good's she going to be locked up at night I . . . ' went on Grandfather.

Before he could finish the sentence, Pablo was on his feet and throwing his arms about both of them. Then he ran to the puppy who was watching, head cocked to one side, and hugged her crying, 'They're not going to chain you up. They're not going to chain you up.'

'Well, well,' laughed Grandfather, pleased in spite of himself to see Pablo so happy. 'I suppose we can always get another dog for the yard.'

'No, Grandfather. She'll be a good guard dog, you'll see. You won't need another one and you can throw the chain away.'

'Well, well,' he repeated, understanding more from the boy's looks than his words.

'This lad!' sighed Grandmother, also with a smile. 'He always gets what he wants from us. He twists us round his little finger. But it won't be like that when your parents come home. You won't get all your own way then.'

For once the thought of his parents' future homecoming meant nothing to him. His puppy was saved from the chain which, all of a sudden, no longer frightened him. Later on, he went out to the yard, walked up to the kennel and took a last look at it. The snow had disappeared from the yard and it lay in puddles and mud, abandoned and useless. He gave it a disdainful kick, which sprayed his trousers with mud, and never thought of it again.

6

Pablo called his dog Neska, a Basque word meaning 'little girl'. He got it from Grandfather who, in his younger days, had fished with a Basque fleet. Sometimes he told Pablo stories about whaling and cod-fishing up in Icelandic waters and Pablo wondered why he had ever left such an exciting life to return to his father's farm.

'He came back to marry me,' laughed Grandmother. 'I wasn't having him chasing whales and cod and who knows what else, and me at home, all alone, not knowing what he was doing or even if he was alive.'

'You could have gone with him, like my parents.'

'On a fishing boat! And, anyway, it was time for him to settle down. Half the tales he tells you aren't true, either. They're fisherman's tales.'

But Pablo still listened to him with unabated admiration, dreaming sometimes of having the same adventures when he grew up.

'It's not the same any more,' Grandfather told him. 'Half the excitement's gone with all the gadgets they have these days. The days for adventuring are over, unless you want to go to the planets.'

Now that he had the puppy, Pablo didn't have so much time to listen to Grandfather's stories. He didn't follow him about the farm half so much, either. When he wasn't at school he was running about the yard with his dog, playing tag, or rolling about with her in the barn, struggling in the straw, imagining he was defending himself from an attack by wolves.

'You wouldn't stand much of a chance if she really was a

wolf attacking you,' Grandfather told him one day. 'A couple of bites from those beasts can tear you to pieces. I remember my father telling me about the state they found a hunter in who'd only gone to shoot rabbits and didn't come back. They could hardly recognize him when they did find him.'

'Don Elicio says wolves don't attack people. He says all those stories about wolves attacking people are legends and imagination.'

'He wouldn't say that if he'd seen the hunter!'

'He says there are wild dogs in the mountains and people think they're wolves, but they're not really. He says he bets it was dogs that attacked the cattle this winter.'

'He knows a lot about wolves for a city man,' said Grandfather with a hint of scorn. 'I don't suppose he's ever seen one.'

'Have you seen a wolf, Grandfather?'

Pablo was sitting up now, pulling bits of straw out of his hair, and the dog was sitting beside him, panting, her tongue lolling out, her eyes bright, ready to start a new attack at the slightest hint from the boy.

Grandfather laughed and pulled Pablo's ear. 'If I say I have, you'll say I was mistaken, that it was a dog.' Then he sighed and went on, 'You're getting too clever for me. Once I could tell you a lot of things, but they teach you so much in that school these days that it'll need your father to keep up with you, not an old fellow like me who was working when he was eight.'

Pablo caught the note of sadness in the farmer's voice. He jumped up, immediately followed by the dog, and said, 'But you've done a lot of things that I'll never be able to do and – whether they were wolves or dogs – you've seen them and the teacher hasn't.'

Grandfather laughed delightedly, rubbing Pablo's hair with his rough hand. 'You're a good lad,' he said, 'but I don't know what your grandmother will say if you go upstairs like that, covered with straw. You'd do better to look for eggs under the straw instead of tossing it about.'

Neska, who had as quickly learned to answer to her name as she had to the previous clicks and whistles, started nosing in the straw beside the boy. He carefully felt about with his hands in the most likely places while she snuffled beside him, pushing her nose under the straw, snorting and sneezing at the dust.

'Do you think she knows I'm looking for eggs?' Pablo asked with a laugh, putting his arm round her neck.

'I don't know, but if she finds any it'll be because she breaks them. She can probably smell a rat or two.'

Grandfather went off to tend the cows, which during the hardest months of winter were chained in their stalls. Pablo liked having them in the barn. Their occasional soft moos, the sound of their chains or their hooves changing position in the straw were a background to all his games. In the summer, when they were out in the fields all day and even milked there, he missed their presence and looked forward to their eventual return.

Soon they would be going back to their pastures. The snow had melted. The nights were still sharp with frost and the days too, sometimes, but Grandfather had been examining the grass and saying that very soon now it would be fit for eating. There had been snowdrops and now crocuses were struggling through in patches on the edges of the forest. Soon there would be bluebells and daffodils. Spring was coming.

Neska was nearly three months old, with giant paws and floppy ears. She was as clumsy as she was playful and knew no difference between herself and the boy. For her, he was mother and brother rolled into one. He fed her and played with her and was often still beside her when she fell into her exhausted baby sleeps. He wasn't always there when she woke up but she had grown used to his absences and no longer cried for his coming, confident almost to the minute of his return.

For a time, Pablo had had to tie her up in the barn when he left her because, bored by his absence, she had tried barking at the cows and then nipping them. Her excited yappings, which grew angrier and more hysterical the less they noticed her, could be heard all over the farmyard and in the house. The cows at last grew ruffled, rattling their chains as they tried to shake their horns at her, and Grandfather came hurrying to see what was happening.

He laughed to see the puppy's fury, which was such that, when he picked her up to pull her out of danger, she attacked his hands with her needle-sharp teeth. The minute he put her down again she rushed back to renew the attack and in the end he had to find a bit of rope to tie her in her place because she was so stubborn and disobedient. That kept her busy for a while, scratching, tugging and gnawing at it, and in the end she fell asleep, but her legs still kicked and she yapped while sleeping.

'The other day she was causing havoc among the hens,' went on Grandmother, when her husband had finished relating the story to Pablo. 'She chased them here, there and everywhere and she wouldn't take the slightest notice of me

until I chased her with the broom. Even then she had the cheek to turn round on me and start biting at it.'

They all laughed and Pablo was proud of these signs of courage in his dog.

'You see,' he said, 'She'll defend us from wolves this winter. She won't be scared of them, not one bit.'

'If there's anything left to defend by the time winter arrives,' replied Grandfather. 'The way she's going on, I'm beginning to doubt it.'

So Pablo tied her up when he left her. If she woke up before he came to release her, she played with her blanket and eventually tore it to shreds. Every day her teeth were sharper. She gnawed at the bones she couldn't yet crack and sharpened them against their hard smoothness, and she filled Pablo's hands with scratches, sometimes bringing tears to his eyes when she nipped him a bit too hard.

'She's getting very unruly,' Grandfather warned him one day. 'She's not such a baby that you can't start teaching her who's master. If you don't learn to control her while she's young she'll never learn anything when she's older.'

The trouble was, Pablo didn't really know how to control her and Grandfather couldn't give him much advice. His guard dogs had always been chained which had made them morose and savage with strangers. It hadn't been necessary to teach them anything. The few things they needed to know they learned at the end of the chain! They soon learned that it was unbeatable and that the only way to defy boredom was by barking at every strange movement or sound. The gun dog was chained in the barn and dashed off like a wild thing when released. He had learned to come when called through sheer fear of the beating he would get if he didn't return, which sometimes had the effect of making him keep away longer than he might have done if he hadn't expected a beating, and he wasn't trained to fetch the animals his master shot. His nose took them to them and sufficient punishment had taught him that he mustn't eat or maul them but just stand and guard them for his master.

It wasn't that the farmer was a cruel man. It was just that

45

he knew no other way of training a dog to obedience and his dog was afraid of him at the same time that he adored him.

The only advice Grandfather gave to Pablo was to hit her hard when Neska didn't do what he expected of her and Pablo, who wasn't a bullying sort of boy at all and had never deliberately hurt anything in his life, just couldn't imagine himself ever willfully hurting Neska. It was true that she sometimes hurt him, but she didn't do it on purpose. She was only playing and she didn't know the strength of her own teeth or the damage they could do.

It wasn't as if she were really bad, either. She was just a puppy and wanted to play with everything, the cows, the hens, the pigeons. The more they kicked or fluttered, the more she wanted to play. The more he wrestled with her, the more she fought back. To him, the answer was in tying her up when he wasn't there to keep an eye on her, and being with her all the rest of the time.

When spring came and there began to be some sunshine after the rain, and high winds began to dry out the soggy fields and winter wet forest, Pablo went exploring with her along the banks of the streams and along the forest's edge. He had never walked through his grandfather's fields with a dog before and the experience was so delightful that, from then on, he never tired of running off with her. Together, they spent hours away from home, Pablo having begged some bread and cheese from Grandmother, often not returning until the westerly fields were tinged with sunset and the forest looked closer and darker.

Grandmother worried about him. To her he seemed a very small boy still, but Grandfather laughed at her.

'You pamper him too much. He's not a girl. When our son comes home I want him to find Pablo a man, not a baby. Besides, he's got Neska with him. He won't come to any harm with her.'

'She's hardly more than a puppy. How she can look after him, I don't know.'

'Huh! If the way she attacks my cows is anything to go by, I'd say a boar or a bear would be all in a day's work to

46

her. The noise she'd kick up would be enough for us to hear it from here. They're not very far away really. It seems a long way to them, and to us, too, because we can't see them, but we'd hear them pretty soon if anything happened.'

'At least he's got company now,' said Grandmother after a pause. 'He seemed so lonely sometimes with no one to play with. That Neska might be only a dog but she makes him happy. He's laughed more since he's had her than ever before. I used to worry about him being so lonely, without boys of his own age, without his mother. . . .'

Grandfather sighed. 'Yes, you're right, woman. We do our best but it's not the same for a boy as if he had brothers or sisters or his own parents. We're too old for him. Perhaps that's why he's such a quiet lad. He doesn't seem like most boys of his age.'

'I don't know. If only our son would come back soon. . . . And when he comes back, do you think he'll stay here with us?'

'Who knows, woman, who knows? But it's no good worrying and getting sad about things we can do nothing about. The boy's happy. So stop worrying about him. He's got Neska, hasn't he, and she's as good as bread to him.'

7

Throughout all the summer Neska went on growing. So did Pablo, according to Grandmother, who spent many an evening sitting in the late sunlight with her sewing basket and the boy's shirts and trousers letting them out. Pablo didn't notice himself growing, except when Grandfather measured him against last summer's notch in the barn door, comparing it with the notch that had been made for his own father at the same age twenty-five years before. He was just a bit taller than his father and that made him feel good. The old notches were worn and looked as though they were part of the wearing wood. Only the notches made over the last five years, since Grandfather had started measuring him, stood out. It was when Grandfather had first started to measure him, explaining about the other notches, that Pablo first learnt that his father had had a sister who had died when she was seven. There were notches for her too, the only visual memory they had of her because there wasn't even a photograph.

Pablo had grown all of two inches since the previous summer but Neska grew much more quickly. Grandfather hadn't been far wrong when he had said she would grow to be as big as a calf because she was already taller than the three-day-old bull calf he brought from the village the same morning that he measured his grandson. Grandfather said she was of mastiff blood, which explained her height and the size of her head. She was not as heavily built as a true-bred mastiff, however. The thick wool of puppyhood had given way to a coat of soft, brindle-grey hair and neither Grandfather nor Pablo had any doubt but that she was the handsomest dog in all the district. Two or three neighbours had offered to buy her and the man who had originally given her to Grandfather cursed himself for a fool, especially when Grandfather reminded him that he had been going to drown her.

She was still too young to have learnt any self-control and dashed about all over the place as soon as Pablo untied her each day. He had to steel himself not to be knocked over by her and now when she jumped up at him she was tall enough to lick all over his face, with her paws on his shoulders. Pablo could hardly believe that she had once been small enough to tuck inside his jersey and not so very long ago. Now he could sit on her back. She didn't like him sitting there and would struggle out from under him, sometimes dumping him on the ground, and when her fast-wagging tail hit him against his legs she really hurt him.

Pablo adored her. She gave him the company he had lacked all this time and now whenever he wrote to his parents his letters were full of news of her. Before he had rarely written them more than a page but now he would fill two or three pages with all kinds of information about her. Grandfather, reading the letter out loud to his wife before folding it carefully to put in the envelope, was often surprised by the amount of things the boy noticed about her. She had brought him to life in a way that nothing else had.

They wandered all over the farm together and beyond, into the forest fringes, and Pablo wrote of the things they saw together, the birds, the squirrels, the clusters of toadstools in the damp shadows. He noticed the birds because Neska startled them, the squirrels because she barked at them, the toadstools because she went lumbering into them, smashing them under her clumsy paws, and he had been afraid she might eat them and die.

It seemed that every day was an adventure to him because he shared it with Neska and he had nothing else to talk about but her. Grandmother wondered if it was right for him to devote so much time to the dog but he didn't neglect his school work, he ate ravenously and his face was bright with colour. Both the grandparents were proud of him and pleased with themselves because he looked so healthy and happy. They felt keenly the responsibility of bringing him up well in his parents' absence but their main worry about him – his loneliness – had been solved, thanks to Neska. The bike, gathering dust in the barn, was forgotten.

That summer Pablo ventured farther into the forest than he had ever done before, except with Grandfather. He had always been afraid of the immensity of the forest land, with its toweringly tall trees, its wilderness of narrow paths that came up against walls of impassable thickets, its darkness in certain places, its silence which was broken with heart-stopping suddenness at the shriek of a bird or an angry squirrel. The knowledge that bears and boars and wolves might haunt those endless, almost untrodden groves which climbed higher and higher, and might be watching him, inspired him with primitive fear.

Although he knew, because Don Elicio had told him, that nearly all the larger wild life had been exterminated, memories of his grandfather's tales and warnings, stories he had read in books and comics, the things the boys said at school, the mangled chickens and the torn bullocks which had been slaughtered by the village butcher because of the gravity of their wounds – he had seen them standing dismally outside the butcher's shop, dogs sniffing round them, children curious, adults impressed and angry – all these made him afraid of the forest and its unseen inhabitants.

But with Neska he was no longer afraid. She was as big as any wolf, braver and stronger, and he knew she would fight for him with the same heat and willingness with which he would fight for her. Afraid of nothing, she was eager to know the forest's every secret and she crashed through undergrowth and bracken, eyes bright with expectation, unaware that the depths were darker, colder and more silent. Pablo followed, forgetting his fear at the sight of her waving tail, and the sound of her heavy, crashing body and her wild, echoing barks as soon as she found anything to bark at, be it only a lizard stiff with fear under a stone.

Rabbits fled, pigeons, crows and other birds Pablo didn't recognize swooped away from her, calling out warnings to all their kind. Once, when they had gone farther than ever into the forest and were high up, near an outcrop of massive grey stone where the sun beat hotly down on them, Neska started up a bird that Pablo had only ever seen from a distance before and that only rarely. It was a falcon, and before it swept out into the air currents, uttering that lonely cat-like cry which could be heard right down at the farm at times, Pablo caught a glimpse of curved beak, sharp black

51

eyes and sun-glossed feathers. Pablo was afraid that Neska would fall over the precipice in her excitement but she had the sense to stop at the edge, though she barked frantically, front legs stiff, tail thrashing excitedly until she convinced herself that it wouldn't return and was too far off to be caught by her.

For the first time since Grandfather had started notching up his height when he was three years old, Pablo was measured twice that summer, the second time when the leaves were beginning to change colour and fall, and school was only a week away. He had grown a whole inch in just those summer weeks and Grandfather said it was because he had spent so much of his time in the forest, trying to grow as tall as the trees.

Soon after Pablo went back to school, Grandfather had to go to the city to fill in some forms. The village bus would take him to the nearest town, from which he would have to take another bus to the city. It was a long way and he would have to set out as soon as he had milked the cows. Grandmother couldn't go with him because someone had to stay behind to look after the animals. Pablo listened to them talking about the journey, planning it as carefully as if it were a journey to the other side of the world. They travelled so rarely that this was quite an event. In the end Grandfather said he was going to take Pablo with him.

'But what about school? He'll miss the whole day!' protested his wife.

'So what? A day in the city is more educational than a whole week at school. He'll see things he's never seen before, except in books. You'd like that, wouldn't you, Pablo?'

They reached the city at about ten the next morning. Its main industry was coal-mining and on its outskirts the emerald green fields and velvety-coloured hills disappeared. Ugly buildings, with black and broken window-panes and looking as drear and dusty as their surroundings, stood out starkly, and the louring sky, which later filled with rain, made everything still darker and sadder-looking. There were some newer, cleaner buildings, which Grandfather said were factories for dairy products, and Pablo looked at everything wonderingly. He had never seen a factory before although he knew his mother and father worked in one.

The houses in the city were taller than the trees in the forest and although some were of brick and some of stone, Pablo saw them all a sad grey colour, with grey blinds half covering curtained windows. The pavements were hard and his legs grew tired as he paced along beside Grandfather who every now and again had to ask a passerby for the street he was looking for. People hardly stopped to answer him. The words flew out of their mouths as they hurried on and Grandfather had to ask again because he didn't understand them. By the time they found the place they were going to, Pablo was wishing he had stayed at home. He was feeling miserable for Grandfather, who was obviously as lost as he was in these strange surroundings and almost childlike in his bewilderment, talking to people who didn't want to listen.

They climbed a dark, wooden staircase and entered a barrack-like room which was lit by glaring fluorescent lamps. The room was divided by a long counter, behind which a number of men dressed in Sunday suits attended the several long queues which crowded the room. They stood in one of the queues for nearly an hour, with nothing to do but stare at the clothes and faces of the people round them, most of whom seemed villagers like themselves. The men behind the counter shouted at nearly everybody – when it was Grandfather's turn they shouted at him too, and made him join another queue – and Pablo wondered why they were so disagreeable if they were rich enough to wear a Sunday suit on a weekday.

There were only two good things about that day in the city as far as Pablo was concerned. One of them was the lunch they ate in a little back-street restaurant near the bus-station. This was an adventure for Pablo because he had never eaten away from home before or been given a menu with a list of meals to choose from. Grandfather didn't have much experience, although he pretended he had, but luckily for both of them the waiter was used to village people. After letting them run their eyes over the menu in a bewildered fashion, he suggested a couple of meals they would be sure to like.

They each had a great plateful of beans stewed with spiced sausage and ham and red pepper with salad to follow and half a bottle of red wine to drink. Afterwards Pablo had an ice-cream with chocolate sauce which he didn't really have room for but which he couldn't resist, while Grandfather watched him with a smile of proud contentment because he knew the waiter was admiring his grandson's appetite, sipping a glass of brandy which his wife would be cross about if she knew. Pablo had promised not to mention it. It was a first-class meal in a first-class restaurant, they were both quite convinced of that, and as Pablo chased the last sliver of melting ice-cream round the glass cup he felt that perhaps the city wasn't so bad after all.

But better than the beans and the ice-cream was when Grandfather stopped at a shop which sold sports and hunting equipment. The window was full of tennis racquets, shotguns, fishing tackle and footballs. On one side a number of chains and leads and dog collars dangled from hooks.

'Just look at that collar!' exclaimed Grandfather, pointing to a thick piece of leather studded with nails. 'That's just what your Neska wants to protect her throat should she ever get into a fight with another dog or a wolf.'

Pablo examined it thoughtfully. It was a powerful, vicious-looking collar.

'Couldn't she hurt herself with it?'

'I don't know how. The only thing to get hurt would be any other dog or animal that tried to attack her. If she wore that round her neck when you go to the forest, your grandmother wouldn't worry so much about you. Besides, she ought to wear a collar. If she gets lost one day, who's going to know that she belongs to anyone? With a collar like that, everyone will know she's got a master.'

54

Grandfather's enthusiasm convinced him. It was a very impressive collar, displayed by itself in front of all the rest. There wasn't a dog in the whole village with a collar like that one. He smiled up at Grandfather, nodding contentedly.

The shop didn't open until five o'clock. The bus left at six. There would be time to buy the collar but they couldn't stand outside the shop for nearly two hours till it opened. Grandfather decided to take Pablo to see the cathedral. He had seen it once before, many years ago, and could hardly remember what it looked like.

'You just see how your grandfather knows where it is. I don't need more than an hour to find my way around a place, even though I'm not as young as I used to be,' he boasted.

It had been raining heavily but now a wind was driving away the clouds and the sun was beginning to shine, flashing on the many window-panes and the windshields of an occasional passing car. There wasn't much traffic at this time in the afternoon, which secretly relieved both of them.

In the cathedral itself the sun shone through the high windows, making patterns at their feet. It made Pablo think of the way it shone through the trees in the forest, and the stone columns reaching up to the vault made him think of the trees themselves. It was the only part of the city that reminded him of his daily surroundings and he felt a warmth there that rid him of the depressing feel of the streets.

He almost fell asleep in the bus on the way home, and so did Grandfather. Neither of them were used to the hardness of the city. Pablo had taken the collar out of its tissue paper and held it in his hands. Every now and again he looked at it, revelling in the smell of its brand new leather and the feel of its sharp-pointed nails. It was the best present he had ever had, except for Neska herself, and he could see Grandfather felt very pleased with himself when he said so.

8

As time went by and Neska left puppyhood behind she became less troublesome about the farmyard. Pablo no longer needed to tie her up when he went off to school. She had tried to follow him sometimes and once had gone all the way to the village with him, waiting for him outside the school till he came out, but she must have realized that there wasn't much fun in it and only did it that once. Pablo didn't know if he was pleased or disappointed. It was very agreeable to have Neska waiting for him, but it was very dull for her and she might get into mischief in the village.

She was used to him going off in the morning and coming back in the afternoon and was usually trotting down the lane to meet him as he came home, tail wagging, eyes bright, the nails of the new collar showing amid the thick hair round her neck. Grandfather said you could tell winter was coming, just by the way Neska's hair grew. It was getting thicker all the time and Pablo could sink his fingers into it and almost hide them from sight.

During the day she might follow Grandfather about the farm or stay at the kitchen door watching Grandmother, attracted by the smell of a stew she might be preparing, chickens she was cleaning, or a rabbit being skinned. She always threw all the bits to Neska, who usually caught and swallowed them before they touched the ground, and as soon as the bones that had made the stock for the stew had cooled sufficiently, Neska would sit for hours cracking them with teeth that had now grown as hard as the bones themselves. She held them between her big front paws, licking and gnawing, her eyes shut with pleasure, and then she would bury them in places that only she knew about. Sometimes she would bury them first and dig them up for eating weeks later.

The hunting dog had a poor life compared with hers because the farmer didn't have time to go hunting very often and, just as he only used his axe when he needed it, so he only made use of the dog when he needed him. The rest of the time he was shut up in the barn sleeping at the end of his chain, his main joy in life being the forty-five seconds needed in which to swallow his daily ration. The farmer addressed a few words to him when he came into the barn and, with sad eyes, he watched the games that Pablo and Neska played there, sometimes whining and jumping about, infected by their excitement.

One evening, when they were having supper round the table, enjoying the warmth of the brazier at their feet and the warmth of the hot soup in their stomachs, Grandfather said, 'You'd better start tying Neska up again before you go off to school in the mornings.'

'Why? What's she been doing?' Pablo was surprised as for a long time now neither Grandmother nor Grandfather had complained about her at all.

'It's not what she's been doing. It's what she will be doing if you don't take care. To my mind, it looks as though she'll be running off to find herself a boy friend one of these days.'

Pablo looked to see if Grandfather was joking. He knew girls had boy friends, when they were grown up, but surely not dogs!

'Yes, son. Your Neska's not a puppy any more. She'll be looking for a mate so that one day she can have a family of her own.'

'That's all we need!' exclaimed Grandmother. 'Now you know why I didn't want you bringing a bitch into the house. There'll be puppies all over the place, not to speak of strange dogs maundering about, perhaps killing the hens and all.'

Pablo hardly heard her, struck by his grandfather's words. Neska having a family of her own! A thrill of excitement shot through him. Neska with puppies must be the most beautiful thing in the world – well, she already was, but she'd be doubly so with puppies. His face was alight with the thought. He remembered how beautiful she had been as a puppy and to think there'd be lots of baby Neskas, all as beautiful as she was and all belonging to him.

'So make sure you tie her up,' Grandfather was saying, breaking through his thoughts.

'But if I tie her up she won't be able to find a boy friend and she won't be able to have puppies!'

'That's just the idea, so don't you go thinking anything else,' agreed Grandmother. 'Lots of trouble will be saved all round if you make quite sure that Neska behaves herself.'

That night Pablo thought a lot about Neska becoming a mother. He thought of the calves and the baby rabbits and the kittens that ran wild about the yard and barn, and how all the animals wanted a mate and a family. And he thought of his own mother and father, whom he didn't often think about these days in spite of the letters they sent and the letters he wrote to them. They were really of so little importance in his daily life now that they almost didn't belong to it at all. Suddenly his heart clenched with pain, the old pain he used to feel sometimes before he had Neska, and he felt so alone and different from the boys at school who went home to their mothers and fathers every day. Would they ever come back as they promised? And would they bring him a brother or sister as he used to hope, before he had Neska?

He went back to thinking of Neska again, so that the pain soon faded. She wouldn't be happy if she couldn't have a mate and a family. She had him but it wasn't enough, so Grandfather said. She wanted a mate and puppies of her own. He would be able to share the puppies with her. It would be as if they were his own family as well as hers. And it wouldn't be right to tie her up and not let her have puppies in spite of what Grandmother said. All the animals on the farm had young, all the animals and birds in the forest. And people were the same. He thought of all the excitement there was in the village when someone got married, or when a baby was born. It was the happiest time for everybody, human or animal, so it must be very important. He went to sleep determined not to tie Neska up.

Hardly a week later, Neska disappeared. Grandfather was very cross with Pablo and Grandmother was cross with both of them. Pablo got sent to bed without any supper for his deliberate disobedience, though Grandmother said it was as much Grandfather's fault because he knew Neska was still running loose. Pablo couldn't sleep for a long time, not so much because he'd been sent to bed hungry and before he was tired, but because he was all the time wondering where Neska was and worrying a bit about her.

He hoped she was enjoying herself, looking for her mate, but supposing something happened to her? Supposing she went to another farm and a farmer shot at her? Suppose she got lost and couldn't find her way home? He was glad she had a strong collar which would protect her against un-friendly dogs or wild animals, at least. But in the midst of his worry he smiled to himself, thinking of the puppies she would one day be mothering.

The next day he saw her in the village, trotting along with several dogs round her. It had been raining all night and she looked dirty but happy. Pablo called her name and went towards her. She looked at him, wagging her tail, her big mouth open as if grinning with happiness. The other dogs looked too and began to shrink back a bit as Pablo came up.

'But Neska, where've you been all night? You've got to go home,' he began, stretching out his hand.

Neska went on wagging her tail but sidled out of his reach. He went to slip his fingers through the collar but she jumped away and in a second she was loping off down the street, followed by her companions, and she didn't even look back when he called her name. She disappeared down an alleyway and when Pablo reached the same corner she was nowhere in sight.

Pablo stood there, surprised and hurt. Never before had Neska ignored him. She had always come when he called, even when she'd done something wrong and knew she was to be punished – with words rather than blows because Pablo had never hit her, in spite of his grandfather's advice. He couldn't believe that Neska could ignore him so completely. He could understand her running away from the farm while she was on her own – after all, he abandoned her every day – but he couldn't understand her running away from him now.

He turned back to school, feeling shunned and alone. He hadn't minded sharing her with a mate, was prepared to do so, but he did mind her no longer wanting him at all. There was a very bitter feeling in his heart all day.

He cheered up towards home time, thinking that by now Neska must surely be back at the farm, and he ran through the rain and the mud and the sharp, north wind, not noticing any of them, forgiving her in the expected warmth of the wild greeting that would be waiting for him. But Neska wasn't there, hadn't been there all day.

He didn't tell Grandfather he had seen her. That was a humiliation he could share with no one, and because he was so silent they both tried to cheer him up by telling him that Neska would soon be back, thinking he was worried about her absence.

'We could go and look for her if we knew where she was,' suggested Grandfather.

'In this weather!' exclaimed his wife.

'If it made the boy happy, why not? I'll be getting a lot more wettings before I go to my rest, but we don't know where she is.'

Pablo didn't say anything but when he was at last alone, in the warmth of his blankets and eiderdown, his heart surged in anger against the dog. For the first time he could imagine himself beating her for her disobedience. There wasn't only pleasure in loving, as now he discovered. There was hurt and anger and humiliation and he had felt them all that day for Neska.

She came back three days later, waiting for him in the yard when he made his first appearance after breakfast. It was still raining, a drizzle that had hardly stopped all these days, and he could hardly recognize her, so bedraggled was she. But there was a light of pleasure in her eyes as she furiously wagged her tail, barking her greeting loud and unrepentingly.

He cried out her name and rushed down the steps to greet her, almost falling. She jumped all over him, covering him with her mud, but he didn't care. He didn't even notice.

After the first face slobberings, he took her to the barn where he rubbed her down with straw and an old sack. She was soaked right through to the skin, while all her underhair, legs and tail were caked with mud. She was ravenously hungry and Pablo rushed to the kitchen to find her something to eat. There was always something in the big pot for the dogs, bits that Grandmother threw in and stewed up throughout the week.

She wolfed down a whole potful of food and then lapped up the morning's milk with which Pablo refilled the same pot. As he watched her, Pablo's heart filled with joy and pleasure. He'd forgotten her treachery, forgotten his pain, in the joy of having her back.

Grandmother said, 'She's back, is she?' adding with a sarcastic tone, 'I wonder what she's brought with her!'

Grandfather said, 'I knew she wouldn't get lost. You shouldn't have worried so. She can look after herself. You know it now, so you needn't worry again.'

The weeks went by. Now, when the clouds became too heavy, snow fell. At first it didn't settle. There were patches of it in the straw in the yard. The rest quickly turned to slush and disappeared, but the mountains were lost in the greyness of the sky and often even the forest was invisible. Pablo still went for walks with his dog but they didn't go very far. It was cold, very cold, and Neska no longer dashed here and there, her eyes begging him to be quick. She trotted along beside him, her breath panting out hot clouds, and was more eager than he was to turn back home.

Soon Pablo could see how fat she was getting. He asked Don Elicio how long it took for dogs to have puppies and was told about two months. He marked a date on the calendar and every day mentally crossed one off. He instinctively felt that Grandmother wasn't pleased about Neska having puppies so he kept off the subject. They said nothing and neither did he. If he wanted to know anything, like how long it took, he asked the teacher.

He asked the teacher if it would hurt her and Don Elicio said no, and that he wouldn't need to worry when the time came round because dogs, like all animals, knew how to look after such things by themselves, preferring to be alone. Pablo wanted to be with her when the puppies were born, partly because he was curious about how it would happen, and partly because he wanted to share this great experience with Neska. He didn't think she would mind, although he had already discovered that in some things Neska preferred to be independent.

The day marked off on the calendar came – and went. Pablo put some fresh straw in the place where Neska slept, twice as thick as usual, and sat beside her most of the day because she didn't seem inclined to move. He brought her a dish with fresh water so that she would have it within reach, but she didn't drink any and soon it was dirty with the dust from the straw. She panted a lot and looked at him with her dark, devoted eyes, into which Pablo tried to read so many thoughts. How many times did he wonder whether she could think as he did but in a more limited way, or whether she never really thought at all? There didn't seem to be any way of finding out. Grandfather said animals didn't think. The teacher said he didn't know but that experiments suggested that certain animals might have some thought process.

Did she know she was going to have puppies, that she was going to be a mother so soon? And how would she know what to do and how to care for them? It was a great mystery to Pablo, one which consumed most of his mind. He was anxious and excited, longing for it to happen soon so that perhaps he could get the answer to some of his questions. He had never actually seen an animal being born and, although he knew the physical details of what would happen, it was still beyond his imagination.

The next day he came running back from school, sure that

the puppies would be waiting for him, but only Neska was there, curled up in her nest, wagging her tail but disinclined to move. He went to school the following morning very reluctantly, knowing that he was going to miss the most important thing in his life, and came racing back in the afternoon again, breathlessly expectant.

Grandfather was waiting for him, smiling in anticipation of the news he had to give. 'They've arrived, they've arrived!' he exclaimed. 'Six of them. One dead, but the rest as right as rain.'

Pablo dashed to the barn. There was Neska, stretched out on her flank, giving suck to five rat-like creatures, with squashed-up faces and midget legs. She wagged her tail when she saw him and he read into her expression one of satisfied, proud motherhood.

He threw down his satchel and sat in the straw beside her, stroking her head, but she was careless of his attentions and quickly turned when one of the puppies squeaked, not even noticing he was there. She growled when he stretched out a hand, wanting to touch one, and Grandfather, who had come up while he sat there, warned, 'Don't try to touch them yet. They're far too new.'

Later he went away to get on with his tasks, but Pablo just sat there in the straw, watching how she licked them and tucked them into her haunches until they could hardly be seen. She curled herself up round them and fell asleep, sighing heavily, and she didn't care one bit as to whether he was there or not. He didn't mind. He was happy for her. She had her family, which was what she wanted, and it was his family too. He knew she would share it with him soon.

At supper time all he could talk about was the puppies. He wanted to write a letter to his parents right away to let them have the good news. Grandmother protested, 'There's other things to write about too, and you haven't done your homework yet.' She seemed cross but she didn't say why and Pablo soon forgot in his excitement.

Grandfather announced, 'Tomorrow I'll go down to the village and see if anyone wants a puppy or two. We shan't be able to keep them here, you know,' he added, looking at Pablo.

'I know that,' he answered. 'We'll have to find homes for them. I'll ask the boys at school. But they're too small just yet. Let her keep them just a while.'

'The longer she keeps them the worse it'll be,' was Grandmother's comment. 'For both,' she went on, without explaining herself further.

'I shan't mind them going away when they're older,' said Pablo. 'And Neska won't always want them, either.'

Before he went to bed he took her a big potful of milk which she drank down very quickly. He wanted to take her outside for a while but she wouldn't move, for all that he called her. He sat beside her again and stroked her head, trying to catch a glimpse of the puppies which were almost completely hidden, and drew back startled when she growled again.

Grandmother was calling insistently so he had to leave her. He gave her one last caress, then went away, smiling to himself.

9

For the next few days all Pablo thought about was the puppies. He was up early in the morning to rush down to them before breakfast, although he could hardly see them in the lamplight, and as soon as he came home from school he dashed into the barn, without even thinking of saying hello to his grandparents first. At school he told Don Elicio all about them, and he wrote a long letter to his parents in which all his delight was expressed.

When Grandfather read the letter out loud, as was his custom, Grandmother grumbled that it was a waste of a stamp. 'They don't want to hear about the puppies. They want to know what you're doing at school and if you pass all your tests.'

She had been in a bad mood ever since the puppies' birth though Pablo didn't know why.

'Don't send it yet then,' he conceded. 'Save it till next week when Grandfather will be writing.'

It was a hard thing for him to say because he wanted them to have the news as soon as possible, so important was it to him, but he could see that for Grandmother it wasn't news worth telling, and she was so very cross. He put the letter on the dresser, behind the jug among other papers already there, so that it wouldn't be forgotten when Grandfather wrote.

He asked nearly everyone at school if they wanted a puppy but most boys already had a dog at home. No one said yes, not even Don Elicio who hadn't a dog of his own. Grandfather asked the farmers, the ones who had so much admired Neska and would surely be interested in her offspring, but they all had excuses for saying no.

'Just what I knew would happen,' grumbled Grandmother that night at the table.

Pablo was secretly pleased because it meant the puppies would be his far longer, perhaps always, and after supper he went very gladly to tell Neska that no one would be depriving her of any member of her family.

She loved them all equally, he could see that, and spent all her waking time cleaning and feeding them, hardly leaving them for an instant. She still wouldn't let Pablo touch them. He was aching for the feel of them in his hands and had tried sneaking in to them while Neska was outside for a while. But her eyes were on him the whole time and, as soon as she saw him return to the barn, she was there before him, tail wagging, but a warning in her eyes.

Grandmother said, 'Those puppies have got to go. She can't keep them and the longer she has them the worse it will be.'

'Yes, yes,' agreed Pablo, not wanting to make her crosser by arguing, and off he would run to look at them once more.

When he came home from school one afternoon and ran to look at them as usual, he just couldn't believe that they weren't there. Neska wasn't there either and the bed where she and her litter had been sleeping only that morning when he left them was completely cold. For the first few seconds, all he could think was that Grandfather had put them somewhere else. It was getting colder all the time. Perhaps Grandmother had relented and was letting them sleep in the kitchen.

Already his heart was beating faster, even as he reasoned this way, because his heart understood more than his head. Grandmother didn't want the puppies and if she'd been going to move them into the kitchen she would have told him so. She wouldn't have moved them herself, and even Grandfather had nothing to do with Neska. She was his dog and he did everything for her. Where was she, anyway?

He ran out of the barn, face flushed, calling, 'Neska, Neska!'

Grandmother came out of the house. She was upstairs on the landing of the steps.

'Pablo!'

The way she called his name confirmed the fear that he wouldn't admit. He didn't know why, but the way she said it sent a stab of pain right through him.

'Come on up,' she called. 'I want to talk to you.'

'Where's Neska? Where are the puppies?' he cried accusingly, his voice harsh as he still fought not to believe. He wouldn't go up the steps.

'Come on up and let me tell you.'

She began to come down the steps and Pablo ran, not wanting to hear her. She wasn't cross any longer but her eyes were sad and her face troubled. It told him everything – everything but why.

He ran away from the farm along the lane and then through an open gate across the fields, leading to the forest. It was almost dark and he splashed through mud and puddles without seeing them. He wouldn't have seen them anyway, for the tears in his eyes. He was torn with pity and regret for the puppies he had never touched, but mostly his heart ached for Neska whose family had been taken from her.

He stopped at the edge of the field where the forest began. The trees were so dark. He could see nothing beyond them. He stared without seeing, panting, suddenly aware of his blocked nose and wet cheeks, growing colder all the time. He heard Grandfather's voice calling his name and his fists clenched helplessly.

He didn't want to answer but he knew he had to go back. He couldn't hate them for what they had done. He loved them too much, but his soul ached with a sense of injustice and he felt the helplessness that sooner or later each child feels when faced with an adult's implacable and incomprehensible decision.

He would have liked to cry like a baby. The sobs ached inside him but they wouldn't change anything. He would have liked to scream out the words that burned in his heart and head, but they wouldn't change anything either, and could only cause hurt to the people who loved him.

'Pablo, Pablo.'

His grandfather's voice sounded anxious and, at last, with a shuddering sigh, he turned his back on the forest and stomped back across the soggy field, already growing crisp with the night's encroaching frost, feeling cold and empty and helpless. Grandfather was waiting for him at the gate. He put his arm round his shoulders.

'Come on,' he said gently. 'Neska's waiting for you. She needs you tonight.'

'But why, Grandfather? Why?' He knew it was stupid to ask, but he had to.

'We thought you'd understand. We thought you knew you couldn't keep them. And if a thing has to be done it's better to do it quickly. It should have been done just as soon as they were born but . . .' He sighed and held Pablo's shoulders tighter. 'Your grandmother and I, all we ever want is to make you happy, and we wanted to see your face when you saw the pups for the first time. We were selfish. We were thinking of ourselves. We should have thought that, this way, both you and Neska were going to suffer more. Us, too,' he added after a pause, and again, 'Us, too.'

'And where's Neska?'

'She's upstairs. If you like, she can sleep with you tonight. But only tonight, mind you, till she forgets.'

'And do you think she'll have forgotten by tomorrow?'

Grandfather didn't answer.

When they got home Grandmother began to scold about the mud on his shoes and trousers, but Pablo knew it was because she was cross with herself more than with him. They followed him up the steps to the house and, as he reached the door, Pablo could hear Neska whining and scratching.

'Be careful not to let her out,' warned Grandfather, but his words didn't prepare Pablo sufficiently.

As he opened the door Neska flung herself through it and dashed down the steps, anxiously whining, her tail wagging because she was pleased to be free. All three watched as she

dashed to the barn, pushing open the door with her nose and wriggling through the narrow opening. Pablo ran after her and found her nosing anxiously in her bed of straw, the nest where until so recently her younglings had slept.

She looked up at him as he approached, her dark eyes begging for an explanation, and she never stopped whining. She didn't greet him or wag her tail but began sniffing about once more, as if dismissing his presence, digging up the straw, yelping, running back and forth in the barn and looking in corners that even she knew were barren but needing to look somewhere because, unlike the boy, she didn't know that it was no good looking.

He called her name and tried to get hold of her, but she was too anxious to heed him and moved restlessly out of his reach. Then she dashed out of the barn and began darting about the yard, all the time whining and yelping in a tone that Pablo had never heard before. He stood helplessly at the barn door, not knowing what to do, unable to speak, the pain he felt for her choking him.

'Get her,' shouted Grandfather from the steps, 'and bring her up here. She'll only upset herself looking about like that. Your grandmother's got something for her to eat. Bring her up and give her a chance to forget.'

As if something to eat was going to make a mother forget her lost younglings, Pablo bitterly said to himself, but he stirred, unwilling to watch her painful search any longer.

She wouldn't come or allow herself to be caught. Every time he got near she side-stepped out of his reach, reminding him of the day she had run away from him in the village. But then it had been a gleam of joy in her eyes. Now they were intent with bewildered anxiety. Couldn't his grandparents understand that Neska could feel like any mother? How could they think that because she was only a dog she didn't love her babies?

The buildings melted into the darkness as Neska went on searching and Pablo went on watching. Several times she rushed back to the barn and came out again. She went all round the yard and halfway down the lane, occasionally staring at Pablo as if asking him, perhaps wondering why he didn't help her look. He could hardly see her now and only the light from the upstairs windows gave a dim glow to the mud in the yard and the dark figure of the never-still dog.

Again Grandfather came to the top of the steps. 'Bring that dog upstairs and stop messing about. You'll catch your death of cold out there.'

'She won't let me get her. She doesn't want to come.'

'The more she looks, the worse it'll be for her, so bring her up and be quick about it.'

At last Pablo managed to catch her. Reluctantly she followed him into the house, dragging against him. And to think how she tried to get indoors with him on other occasions! For a while she flung herself down near the table where the family was gathered, but she was too restless to stay still for long. She kept getting up and pacing to the door, whining and scratching to be let out. She didn't look at the plate of warm food Grandmother put down for her, or the milk which she usually loved, and nothing would stop her whining. It wasn't a loud protest, just a soft crying sound in her throat.

In the end Grandmother cried, 'For heaven's sake, take her downstairs and tie her up in the barn. I can't listen to her any longer.'

'She can't help crying,' Pablo replied hotly. 'Wouldn't you cry if someone had stolen your babies?'

The words were out before he could stop them. Grandmother looked as though she were going to reply very angrily, but she turned away and said nothing.

It was Grandfather who took Neska downstairs and tied her up in the barn. While he was gone Pablo found the letter he had written to his parents, waiting behind the jug where he had put it a few days earlier. He tore it up and left the bits on the table. He no longer wanted to tell them about the puppies.

When he was in bed he could still hear Neska crying in the barn, her voice rising to a howl then falling to a sob. He pushed his head under the pillow, trying to deafen the sound, and at last he allowed himself to cry, too, crying for Neska who had trusted him, crying because sometimes the world was too cruel a place to bear. He fell asleep crying and, if Neska cried all night, he didn't know.

10

Neska forgot about the puppies and, a bit later, so did Pablo. At first Neska's dugs were swollen with milk but Grandfather said that if she didn't have water for a couple of days or anything to eat the milk would dry up. So it was. She wasn't hungry and didn't worry about not being fed but she was tremendously thirsty and even licked the cold stone floors.

'She would have been a good mother,' Grandfather said with a sigh. It was the only comment to escape him that made Pablo think he regretted what he had done.

They didn't talk about the puppies any more. Soon it was Christmas and Pablo was getting out the boxes of figures again, recalling as he did so that soon he would have had Neska for a whole year. She must have been born a few days after Christmas so soon it would be her birthday. Don Elicio said that dogs aged seven years for every year in a man's life and Pablo tried to work it out. According to that theory she was seven years old, but humans didn't have families when they were only seven. She was full grown and yet as puppyish as ever. He gave up trying to work out how old she was when he realized that she didn't care and it didn't matter anyway.

This year he didn't expect his parents to come home suddenly as a surprise. He too had done some growing and he knew now that they would come when they were ready, not when he wanted them to. Grandfather had told him that they were both working in a big factory in Germany and earning a lot of money. When they had saved enough they would come back home.

'Enough? How much is enough?' he had asked.

'Enough to buy somewhere to live.'

'But can't they live here, with us? There's plenty of room here.'

'They went away because there wasn't enough room. Where would they sleep? You sleep in their room and there aren't any more rooms in the house.'

Pablo couldn't imagine living anywhere except where he had always lived.

'Couldn't they build a new house, here on the farm? Santiago's parents have built one. I've seen it. They've even got a bathroom, and taps with water.'

'You can tell them about Santiago's house when they come back home. They might think it's a good idea.'

Often Pablo trudged round the farm with Neska, the snow reaching to the top of his boots sometimes. Neska sank into it right up to her belly but her thick, bear-like fur kept her warm. She looked like an immense wolf from a distance, and the more Pablo looked at her the more he loved and admired her.

He studied the farm from all angles, wondering which would be the best place for his parents to build a house. He could help them with it. He'd helped Santiago's family, who had built the house between various uncles and cousins. He and Santiago and half a dozen boys from the school had spent hours collecting stones for the concrete floors. They had helped stack up bricks brought on a truck from the city, and he had listened while the men talked about pipes and electric wiring and the staircase. He knew he would be able to help his father and, though he was now too old to pretend they would suddenly return like magicians in a story book, he was still hopeful enough to imagine himself helping his father with bricks and cement and window frames.

When the teacher had found out about Santiago's new house, he had taken the whole school one day to watch how it grew, and then they had talked in the classroom about how houses were built. They had all done a project on how they would build a house and when Pablo drew his picture, colouring it with care, he had really planned it thinking of his father and how he would be able to help him.

He and Neska didn't go into the forest in winter. First of all Grandfather had told him he mustn't and secondly it wasn't such a nice place to visit at that time of year. Half the trees were cold and naked and there was almost a sinister aspect about the conifers with their fog-shrouded green. The bracken was brown and soggy and even the berries on the holly bushes seemed malignant in their brightness, tempting but poisonous. Once he and Neska found the tracks of an animal which could have been a dog or a wolf. They followed them for a while, Neska not particularly interested. They had obviously lost all scent and meant nothing to her, but Pablo remembered the raiders of the year before and wondered if this was the very first sign of them.

He told his grandparents about the tracks and once again they warned him not to go into the forest. Grandmother began to worry about her chickens and the men in the village brought their livestock into the barns at night, just in case.

Although Pablo studied his grandfather's farm from all angles, in the end he realized that the only good place for building a house was exactly where the house was already built. In his next letter to his parents he told them that they could either build a new house beside the existing one or add a few rooms, offering his knowledge and assistance. When he wrote the letter he hadn't really thought about the reply they would send him. In his heart he recognized that it was only an idea which they would probably ignore. They ignored so many of the things he wrote in his letters. Mainly they told him to be obedient to his grandparents, to study hard and get good marks at school and to eat well and grow big. They never said anything about Neska, even though he filled his letters with news of her doings.

When a reply came from Germany, Grandfather read it out loud as was his custom. Grandmother couldn't read and Pablo couldn't always understand his father's writing. He would never admit, even to himself, that his father's handwriting was very bad and full of spelling mistakes. Grandfather could understand it perfectly and so Pablo preferred to listen to the words, making pictures in his mind, the same as Grandmother did.

The letters always started the same way, with greetings and words about everyone's health. Grandfather read them as if he never knew what was coming next although Pablo knew them by heart and was impatient to hear the main body of news.

'Tell Pablo to start thinking about building that house, as we have decided to come back home some time in the spring. And tell him to make his bedroom big enough to share with a brother or sister, because that is what his mother is going to bring him back from Germany as a present for being so good all this time.'

Grandmother gave a cry and burst into tears, Grandfather kept saying, 'It can't be true, it can't be true,' and Pablo just sat looking at the pair of them, feeling as they felt but unable to utter a sound. Then Grandmother hugged him, still crying with joy, her tears brushing his cheek, while Grandfather told her not to be foolish and to stop crying.

'My son. My son. He's coming home. At last he's coming back home,' she whimpered, wiping her eyes with the corner of her apron, and Pablo suddenly saw how old she was.

It was only a flash, that sudden look of need and helplessness expressed on her face, but it frightened him. Grandmother was as strong as the oak trees, as solid as the mountain rock, as constant as the sun and the rain. For a second all that was changed and it was a second that pierced right through to his heart. No longer was she just Grandmother. She was suddenly a person that he hardly really knew, and for some reason he was frightened, as if he had suddenly woken up from a dream.

In that moment he forgot all about the good news, so affected was he by the discovery he had just made, and he looked at Grandfather almost fearfully, wondering whether he would be different too. To his relief he looked just the same, smiling with pleasure, laughing at his wife as he so often did, especially when she nagged him, and then he stared at Pablo and said, 'Well, my son, at long last those parents of yours have had some sense. With a bit of luck they'll be back in time to help me with the spring sowing.'

'You and your spring sowing! Do you think they're coming back for that? You haven't seen them in years and all you can think of is having an extra hand on the land.'

'I'm joking, woman. Always moaning!' he exclaimed, winking at Pablo. 'But you haven't heard the rest of the letter yet. Let's see what else they say.'

The rest was an anticlimax, with explanations of why they couldn't come sooner and why they wouldn't come later, to which Pablo hardly listened. So much had occurred in so few seconds that everything seemed a dream. His parents were coming home, his mother was going to have a baby, they were going to build the house on the farm and, somehow, Grandmother was different.

While his grandparents went on talking he excused himself and ran down to Neska who was waiting for him as always in the barn, her eyes warm with love, her tail generating cold air. He sat in the straw beside her and gave her the news, fondling her ears and running his fingers through her coat as he did so.

'I'm going to make you very beautiful for when my parents come home,' he told her. 'You've got to be clean and good and when we've got our new house you can come and live in it, too. I bet my mother will let you sleep in the kitchen if you show her how good you are. And you'll be able to look after my sister.'

For some reason Pablo had fixed in his head that the baby was going to be a girl. He didn't want a brother though he didn't know why. He wanted a little girl that he and Neska could look after between them.

'And you know what we're going to do tomorrow,' he told her. 'Tomorrow we're going to start collecting stones to make concrete. We'll get a big pile so that when my father comes home, all he'll have to do is just pour on the cement.'

Neska wagged her tail in the straw and licked his nose.

Pablo wasn't the only one who had ideas about preparing

76

things for the spring. Grandmother remembered the old cot which was stored somewhere in the barn and she made Grandfather get it out. He said there was plenty of time but she nagged and nagged till he had to leave his other jobs and find it. Pablo helped him look. It was lost beneath old sacks and ropes and canes.

'We haven't used it since you were a baby,' he grumbled. 'It'll need a coat of paint. You can paint it, Pablo, that is, if we find it.'

He pulled aside a broken cartwheel as he spoke. Neska helped, too, by pouncing about in the disused stall where all the junk was, barking now and again as if sensing that something different was happening.

At last the cot appeared, laced with dust and cobwebs. To Pablo it didn't seem to be the sort of place in which to lay a newborn baby and his face must have expressed his thoughts.

'It's a good cot,' protested Grandfather, dragging off a few cobwebs with his hands. 'Your father slept in that when he was a baby and then – and then his sister, who rests in peace.' He crossed himself as he said this. 'It was made out of oakwood, when your father was born. It'll last a century. You've slept in it and now it'll be the little one's turn. About time too,' he added.

'The spiders will have to be got rid of first,' Pablo suggested.

'Bah, there's nothing that a good scrub with a bucket of lye water can't put right. That's your grandmother's job. You go down to the village and buy some varnish. It'll look as good as new long before your little brother or sister will be needing it.'

The cot was scrubbed and varnished, and Grandmother set about knitting a beautiful white shawl with the softest wool. She sat at night with the wool on the table and Pablo felt how soft it was. He had never felt anything so soft, except Neska's fur when she had been a puppy. She finished the shawl and started to make some baby clothes, tiny vests and dresses which looked to Pablo as though they wouldn't fit anything. Surely a baby couldn't be so small! All day long these days she was sewing and knitting, or embroidering small sheets of the finest linen with flowers and little ducks and any pretty thing which occurred to her. Pablo hadn't known she was so clever.

Meanwhile, his pile of stones was growing. Some of them he had dug up from under the snow. Some of them he had brought from the river bed, freezing his hands to get them out. Neska helped him by clawing at the ground and loosening the frozen earth round them. It was hard work and sometimes it looked as though there would never be enough, even for half a room, let alone the floor of a whole house. But when he saw how the pile of tiny things for his sister grew, how the cot shone with new varnish and how Grandfather suddenly found the energy to start putting to right all the things he had gradually been neglecting, so that his son should find the farm in a well-ordered condition – the gates hanging well on their hinges, the broken hutches properly repaired – Pablo knew that the pile of stones would also be sufficient by the time they eventually came home.

I I

The best day Pablo had ever spent, as far as he could remember, had been the previous winter when Grandfather and the other farmers had hunted through the forest for the wolves which had attacked their livestock. The warmth and gaiety of that evening, when Grandmother had generously brought out her best smoked ham and cider, seemed to increase each time he remembered it. With the addition of Neska the following morning, he could say that he had never been happier, but the day his parents came home was far, far better.

No one knew exactly what time to expect them. They were coming by car because Pablo's father had bought one in Germany with some of the money he had saved, and Pablo spent his time restlessly between the house and the lane, watching out for them. He was supposed to be at school but nobody really expected him to go that day, least of all Pablo, and Neska was delighted to have his company.

Grandmother was cooking as she had never cooked before. With the excuse that they must be hungry after the long drive from Germany, she was determined to cook each and every one of her son's favourite meals, which he couldn't possibly have tasted since he left home so long ago. She made big meat pies and boiled a ham, and a delicious smell pervaded the whole atmosphere of the house and yard. All the cats placed themselves strategically about the door, some hiding under the staircase, some sitting on the roof, the more daring ones only a few yards away.

Grandfather killed the two piglets he had been fattening since winter, and they were slowly roasting in the oven, with a dish of apples underneath them. He filled a dozen bottles with cider from the barrel in the barn and Pablo helped him carry them upstairs.

Grandmother gave him a cloth and told him to wipe the best glasses, which were dusty because they weren't used very often, and he sat on the divan which Grandfather had set up in the room that morning and where he would sleep for the first time that night. His room had been got ready for his parents and the cot for the baby was already placed beside the bed. He had stood looking at it for some time that morning, wondering what it would be like when there was a baby in the house belonging to him.

The weather had been very rainy with few signs of spring, but that day it seemed as though even the weather was going to welcome his parents home. The funny thing about spring was that it crept up unawares. One day the countryside was bleak and dead and unpromising, the branches stark, the ground soggy, the hedgerows bare, and then suddenly there were small swellings of promised life in the trees and hedges, and in the sun and shadow over the meadows there was a new green tint. It was like that the day Pablo waited for his parents. He suddenly saw buds which he knew hadn't been there the day before and there was a warmth in the sun which he hadn't felt since autumn.

It wasn't until the afternoon that the little light blue Volkswagen, its roof crowded with suitcases, turned into the lane and jerked its way over the ruts and stones up to the farmhouse. Pablo and Neska danced excitedly round it all the way, the boy waving his arms, the dog barking, and Pablo's father pressed the horn a dozen times in greeting, which brought Grandmother and Grandfather out to the yard to wait for them and made Neska bark louder than ever. She wasn't used to cars and tried to bite the tyres.

Pablo suddenly felt shy when at last, after so much dreaming and hoping, his parents were actually standing before him. He wanted to throw himself into their arms but suddenly he couldn't. He just stood there, looking at these two strangers who weren't strangers, not knowing whether to call them 'Mother' and 'Father' or 'Mama' and 'Papa'.

The two latter words were almost unused by him and he felt shy of pronouncing them. But then his mother cried out his name and enveloped him in a ferocious hug, smothering his face with so many perfumed kisses that she left him in a daze. Neska barked as never before. She sensed that something strange was taking place. Her tail wagged wildly, beating against everyone's legs, and she barked to the air as if to let the whole world know of her excitement.

Then Pablo was hugged by his father, who almost crushed his ribs in the process, and everybody was talking and crying at once, Grandmother using the corner of her apron again to wipe away her tears, his mother using a handkerchief. Pablo watched, proud with contentment, as the two men hugged each other silently and, although he had no intention of crying like the women, there was such a feeling of joy in his heart that swelled up like the yeast that Grandmother used to make bread, wanting to burst out everywhere, that it seemed his body wasn't big enough to hold it.

The details of that day could never be remembered. There was so much talk and laughter, tears and shouts, with cases being unpacked and things being shown, and presents for everybody including a big earthenware bowl for Neska with her name written on it. They did know she was important, after all. While the women looked at the cot and the baby clothes, Pablo's father went to the barn to look at the animals which were Grandfather's pride. Pablo took the opportunity to show him Neska properly. He knew she was the best dog in the village but wanted to hear his father say so.

'She's very beautiful. There's no doubt you've reared her well, and all by yourself, too, which makes her more of a credit to you. I bet there's not a dog in all Spain or Germany as beautiful as she is.' Glorious words which made Pablo's face shine with pleasure.

Grandmother made everybody eat too much. They sat round the table for hours, warm with food and cider and each other's company. Pablo eyed with contentment the big pile of bones which he would later take to Neska. He thought he would burst if he ate any more, but he went on, hardly knowing what he put into his mouth as he listened to the never-ending conversation and joined in when he could.

After the meal, Pablo's mother said she must lie down for a while. She was tired after so much travelling. Grandmother was over-solicitous, thinking of a hundred things she might need and insisting on her having every one of them, ending up by just giving her a bottle filled with hot water because the sheets were damp.

The afternoon was closing in. The forest was already dark and only the house and its immediate surroundings still seemed to catch the sunlight. Grandfather had to tend the animals and when Pablo's father offered to help he waved him away, telling him to go for a walk with Pablo to see how the farm was progressing. They walked for an hour, Pablo hardly pausing for breath as he rushed to tell his father everything that had happened in the last five years, for once forgetting Neska – except to talk about her. She chased back and forth in her usual way, cocking her head on one side at times as if she realized that she didn't have his full attention and not knowing why.

Pablo found his father more real than the photos and letters and far more satisfying. He was tall and solid, easily as strong as the father of any boy in the village, bigger than Grandfather and with a way of talking which made him think of Don Elicio. He treated him as an equal, as a friend. He talked in a way different from Grandfather's, a way which Pablo could feel without understanding and which made the years of separation seem like nothing.

When they returned he went to talk to his mother, who was sitting up in the bed in which he had slept for years, unable to get up because Grandmother refused to let her.

'When is my sister going to be born?' he wanted to know.

'Soon now. In about two months' time.'

'What are we going to call her?'

'I don't know yet. How do you know she's going to be a girl, anyway? Wouldn't you rather have a brother?'

He shook his head. 'I want a sister so I can look after her. Neska's going to help me. She had puppies, you know.

Grandfather said she would have been a good mother only . . . Well, he said she would have been a good mother. She's going to help me look after her.'

'That's nice.'

They stared at each other. Pablo didn't really know what to say to her. He thought she was very pretty, and very different from the women in the village. She looked more modern than they did, with carefully arranged hair, make-up and the hint of flowers in her perfume. Somehow she didn't fit into the idea he had formed of her, a fusion of lamplight and gentleness. She was pretty enough for him to fall in love with but she didn't seem like a mother.

'You're very pretty,' he said at last, wanting to say a lot more but not finding the words as he had with his father, and then he hurried away, overcome with shyness.

That night half the people from the village came to welcome Pablo's parents back and the food that hadn't been eaten at midday disappeared before they went away. Grandfather had to fill all the bottles from the cider barrel again and this was a good excuse for all the men to follow him to the barn to talk and drink there, while all the women crowded round Pablo's mother to talk about the expected baby and what customs and fashions were like in Germany. The children divided their time between the two groups, running about in the yard in spite of the cold, and Neska had to be tied up because she objected to so many strangers about the place.

At long last the wonderful day ended. Pablo was tucked into the divan in the living room by his mother, who gave him a kiss on the forehead before going to the bedroom. Grandmother turned out the oil-lamp on the round table and kissed him too. He heard them all getting into bed, murmuring, yawning, sighing, and the beds creaking as they made themselves comfortable, his parents in the room on one side, his grandparents in the room on the other, and he fell asleep with a smile on his lips, thinking of them all, for once not thinking about Neska whom he had forgotten to untie in the barn.

12

For the next few days everything was very strange. Pablo couldn't get used to the idea of his mother sitting at the table having breakfast with him, or seeing his father come up the steps behind Grandfather, having helped him milk the cows. He had to go back to school but for once he was impatient in the classroom and hardly heard what the teacher said. This was unusual for Pablo, who looked on Don Elicio with a fondness and admiration which some of the boys ridiculed. The teacher noticed his distraction but said nothing, smiling to himself at the boy's happiness. He knew that Pablo often came to him when his grandfather failed him because his father hadn't been there to help him and he knew that, for the moment, there could be nothing in his head and heart beyond the intense excitement and happiness he was living through.

When Pablo wasn't at school he was round his mother or father every minute of the day, endlessly asking questions or pouring out all his stored up memories of things there had never been room or time for in the letters he had written. He still went on with his collection of stones, picking them up and putting them in his pockets every time he came across a loose one lying here or there, and one afternoon, with great ideas and hopes, he took his father to see them. They were piled in a corner at the back of the house. They had seemed a lot when Pablo looked at them by himself, but when he took his father there didn't seem so many after all, perhaps not even enough for the floor of a single room.

'And what are these for?' his father asked.

'For the house I'm going to help you build,' and Pablo

immediately rushed into an explanation, describing all the details of Santiago's house and how he had helped and how everyone in the village would be only too glad to help them, too.

His father said nothing while he spoke. He looked at the stones, hours of work and dreaming, and then, when Pablo had finished and was obviously waiting for him to say something, he sighed.

'The truth is, Pablo, I don't know if your mother and I are going to stay on the farm. We've got to do a lot of thinking before we decide anything, but it's no good talking about building a house here until we make up our minds.'

'You're not going to go back to Germany, are you?' he cried, his heart suddenly beating rapidly with fear.

'No, of course not.' He laughed and tousled Pablo's head. 'But your mother wants to have a nice place to live in, something modern, especially now we're going to have the baby. She doesn't want to have to fetch water from the river every time she has to wash the baby's diapers, or –'

'I'll fetch it for her,' cried Pablo, 'and, anyway, in Santiago's house they've put running water. They've got taps and even a bathroom.'

'Well, we'll see, we'll see. But don't say anything to your grandparents. We don't want them worrying too soon, do we?'

Pablo shook his head, pleased that his father should confide in him but, at the same time, disconcerted by his words. He couldn't imagine living anywhere except where he was and he wasn't sure if his parents meant to go away without him again, though he couldn't believe that they would. His sense of joy was slightly tarnished. Everything had been too perfect, too good to be true. He couldn't really take in the meaning of his father's words, so far were they from the reality he believed in.

'Shall I keep on collecting stones, just in case?' he asked, looking at him hopefully.

'If you want to. I expect they'll be useful, one way or another.'

But Pablo didn't collect any more. The way his father answered told him that he didn't believe in the idea very much.

It was perhaps a result of this new knowledge that Pablo began to notice an atmosphere in the house that hadn't existed at the beginning. His mother and grandmother weren't getting along together as well as they had during the first few days. They argued about a lot of things. Grandmother liked to have her own way. She wanted to treat her daughter-in-law like a child, fussing over her and even scolding her the way she did with Pablo and with her son. Pablo's father didn't mind. He was out with Grandfather most of the time anyway, leaving the two women alone in the house, and he only laughed when his mother talked to him as if he were about Pablo's age. But Pablo's mother did mind. She wanted to be responsible for her husband and son, while Grandmother wasn't prepared to concede one inch of responsibility to her.

'You just rest as much as you can. You'll have plenty to do when the baby comes along,' she would keep saying, but Pablo's mother was used to working eight hours a day in a factory and keeping her home clean at night. She didn't want to rest all day and watch other people do the work.

She wasn't happy in the country. This Pablo soon discovered when he tried taking her for walks across the fields and into the forest. She kept asking how far it was and kept twisting her ankles in the ruts. Once she stepped in a cow pat and made what seemed to Pablo a terrible fuss about such an ordinary occurrence. After that she wouldn't go for walks any more. She objected to Neska jumping up at her and hated the mud in the yard which splashed her stockings. The years in that German city had completely transformed her and, at heart, every day in the little stone house was a misery to her.

All these things Pablo saw and sensed and he worried for his mother, whose very difference made her so attractive to him. He thought of Santiago's mother, robust, red-faced who only wore stockings when she went to Mass, and the village women who wore clogs when they helped with the farmwork, and he knew that his mother didn't belong on the farm, just couldn't be one of them.

They were days when Pablo hardly thought about Neska. For so long there had been nothing in his life but her; all his waking hours had been centred on her; but now he had a dozen thoughts in his head and as many different feelings in his heart. He wanted to be near his mother almost constantly and she wouldn't have the dog anywhere near her, while when he was with his father he was so busy talking to him or listening to him that he hardly remembered Neska nearby, watching him with her usual devotion in spite of his forgetfulness.

Instead of running straight to look for Neska as soon as he got home from school, he ran straight to look for his father or mother and, if the dog missed his company, his grandparents missed it, too. They understood that Pablo should want to be with his parents more than with them. It was perfectly natural. They told themselves and each other this a dozen times a day, but each one felt sore at heart and, suddenly, a little bit lonelier. Neska became more independent. She roamed off on her own to look for rabbits and bark at squirrels but not usually wandering far beyond the limits of her walks with Pablo. There were days when Pablo hardly saw her, except to shout out, 'Hello, Neska,' as he ran up the steps to the house and passed her in the yard.

He didn't notice when she was absent from the farm for several days because more than once he forgot to feed her and Grandmother had to remember both dogs. She just ladled their food into their bowls and left them to eat it or not as they chose, so she didn't notice either. Neska ran about the village lanes and countryside with half a dozen dogs beside her, returning home exhausted and happy, but not even missed.

The weeks went by. Pablo's parents declared that they were going to buy a flat in the city – that grey mining city which Pablo had visited with Grandfather an age ago. They went off in their little blue car to look at flats, sometimes taking Pablo with them, and then they spent hours looking at displays in furniture shops, deciding what they could afford to buy. Pablo's father talked of finding work in one of the city's factories. A friend of his had spoken to the manager and it was only a matter of time before he would be given a place.

It was only a matter of time for the baby to be born, too, and this also brought about its disagreements. Pablo's mother wanted to have the baby in the city hospital. Grandmother said it was a waste of money when it could be born perfectly well in the farmhouse with the assistance of a midwife, or doctor if necessary. Nobody in the village went to the hospital to have a baby. Hospitals were places for people who were sick. Pablo's father made enquiries at various hospitals and clinics and found that it was going to be very difficult to get a bed, perhaps impossible. The argument went back and forth in the evening across the table while they sat with their feet over the brazier, the remains of the evening meal before them, Pablo silent, feeling crushed inside.

He didn't know who he loved more, his parents or his grandparents, and his loyalties were torn between them. His mother cried and he hated everybody for making her cry, and then he found Grandmother weeping silent tears in the kitchen and he felt like crying too.

'Your parents are going to go away,' she told him. 'And they'll take you with them and we'll be alone. We won't have anybody.' She gripped his arm. 'You don't want to go, do you? Tell them to stay. We'll build them the house. They'll stay if you ask them to. You'll ask them, won't you?' she begged him.

Pablo nodded miserably. He didn't want to leave his grandparents and yet he wanted to be with his parents. Everything would be so simple if they built the new house and they all stayed together. But then he thought how much they argued, how many unsaid words hung in the air, making everyone uncomfortable, and he didn't know what he wanted.

At last, in his unhappiness, he remembered Neska. He went to look for her, wanting only to sit beside her in the straw of the barn and pour out all his feelings, filled with a sense of guilt as he realized how little he had thought of her these last few weeks. Why, he couldn't remember having even seen her for several days. He had taken her neither food nor water, nor played with her, nor cared about her, and he ran to the barn, his heart suddenly filled with love for her and intentions not to forget her again.

She wasn't there. He went out to the yard and called her. It was dark and he could see nothing in the shadows beyond the light from the house. Could she be wandering about the fields at this time of night? Surely not. But where could she be then? His mind went chasing back to when he had last seen her. When was it? A few hours ago, yesterday, or the day before yesterday? He just couldn't remember.

He ran upstairs to Grandfather who was plaiting some rope in a corner of the living room.

'Grandfather, have you seen Neska? I can't find her. She's nowhere about.'

'Now you mention it, I don't remember having seen her today.'

He looked into Pablo's anxious face. 'You've been neglecting her a lot lately, haven't you? That's no way to treat a friend.'

'What can I do?'

'Well, it's too dark to look for her now. Wait till tomorrow. She'll be here by then. Perhaps she's only in one of the fields rabbit hunting.'

'But I called her and she didn't come.'

'Don't worry. She'll be back. Besides,' he added confidently, 'nothing can happen to her. She's big enough to defend herself against anything, and with that collar of hers . . . '

That same night the baby was born. Pablo was awakened by someone lighting the lamp in the living room where he slept. Both his father and grandfather were there with their clothes pulled on hurriedly over their pajamas.

'You go back to sleep,' his father told him 'You'll have your brother or sister by morning but meanwhile go back to sleep and don't be a bother to anyone.'

Pablo shut his eyes and tried to sleep but the news had startled him into wakefulness and the light shone in his eyes. There were comings and goings all the time, with Grandmother in her nightdress and black shawl, and the doctor who left his instrument case on the round table. He could hear his mother groaning in the next room and was frightened for her, but the doctor talked to the two men in a jolly fashion and seemed quite unworried, so he supposed it must be all right. They hardly remembered him at all, except for a few minutes when his father sat on the bed beside him.

'It's tough, being a mother,' he said. 'But don't you worry. It'll soon be over.'

'When can I see my sister?'

'Tomorrow morning. Now go back to sleep and don't be a bother.'

Pablo stuck his head under the bedclothes but he couldn't sleep. He remembered when Neska had her puppies and the gay expression in her eyes as she looked at him with her mouth open, panting, seeming to grin with happiness. He wondered if a newborn human baby would be as screwed-up looking as those puppies had been, with no room for eyes and their ears flattened against their skulls. He must have fallen asleep for the next thing he knew was being startled into wakefulness again by a cry, loud and protesting.

He sat up, rubbing his eyes. The light was still burning but there was nobody in the room. Perhaps he had imagined the sound because it didn't come again. But suddenly there were loud exclamations and laughter, and there was Grandmother bustling the men back to the living room.

'But – you awake!' she cried in a scolding tone when she saw Pablo.

'Let him be,' retorted his father. 'It's not every day that there's an addition to the family. Pablo,' he cried, pulling him up in his arms and hugging him. 'You've got what you wanted – a little sister, as beautiful as anyone could wish. Do you want to come and see her?'

'Leave the boy. He can't see her now,' scolded Grandmother.

'I want to see my mother,' he said. 'I want to see her.'

His father carried him into the bedroom as if he were a baby and set him on the floor beside the bed. There was a big oil-lamp on the bedside table by whose light he could see his mother, pale, tired-looking but with a smile in her eyes just like Neska's. He put his arms round her neck and hugged her. He felt like crying, he didn't know why, except that he knew he loved her.

'Out of here, out of here!' cried the midwife. 'Your mother's got to sleep.'

Pablo just had time to glimpse a small shape in the cot before he was whirled out of the room by his father. They found Grandfather setting some brandy glasses on the table, watched by the doctor. 'This calls for a celebration,' he explained as he opened the bottle and poured a little in each glass.

'Me, too!' cried Pablo.

'You! You can't drink brandy!' exclaimed Grandmother.

'Let him have a sip out of my glass,' said his father. 'Just a sip. After all, it's a very special occasion.'

They toasted the new baby, and its mother's health, and Pablo coughed and nearly choked over the sip of brandy which tasted worse than any medicine the doctor had ever prescribed for him. They all laughed at him and sent him back to bed, warm with the happiness shared by them all.

13

The birth of Pablo's sister seemed to bring about a truce in the family. The house was suddenly full of a feeling of happiness again and Pablo was about the happiest person in it. He spent most of the next morning gazing at the tiny baby whose scarlet face was as screwed up as he had expected. The clothes Grandmother had made for her, and which to him had seemed far too small, were actually too big. The sleeves of the little jersey had to be rolled back and her head seemed to disappear in the neck of the embroidered dress. She had very little hair, just a gingery wisp, and when on one occasion she opened her eyes he could tell that they couldn't really see anything yet.

He was longing to hold her in his arms but both his mother and grandmother told him it was too soon, that she was far too small for him to touch.

'But I want to look after her. She's my sister, remember.'

When he came out of school people asked him about his sister. He gave a minute description of her to everyone who asked, certain there was no baby in the world like her, and somebody gave him some sweets for himself and a rattle for his sister with which he rushed home very proudly.

He had forgotten all about Neska again and only remembered, with a guilty start, when he was in bed that night. He wondered where she could be and if she was cross with him. Perhaps she felt that he no longer needed or wanted her and kept out of his way, but he rejected this idea immediately. She would never forsake him, no matter how badly he treated her, he was sure of that. Then where was she? Where was she?

He was so tired, he had slept so little the night before and there had been so much excitement, that he drifted off into sleep still thinking about her. At some time in the darkness he awoke, sure that he had heard a dog barking. He strained his ears but heard nothing. Perhaps he had dreamt it. For a moment he was tempted to get up, but the room was cold and in complete darkness, with the shutters across the windows. He might make a noise and wake up the baby – something he had already been told he must try not to do – and after a few minutes he went back to sleep.

The next day he decided to look for Neska, but first he had to go down to the village for his mother, to bring some things for the baby from the chemist's. While he was in the village he asked several people if they had seen his dog but everyone shook their heads or shrugged their shoulders. He himself wandered up and down the various lanes and looked into people's yards. He even peered through the chinks in the barn doors, wondering if someone might have locked her up, but there was no sign of Neska anywhere.

That afternoon he crossed and recrossed Grandfather's fields, visiting all the places he had ever gone to with Neska, calling her name, cupping his hands round his mouth to make the sound carry farther. At one place it echoed back to him from the hills but no Neska appeared, wagging her tail, her brown eyes laughing. The sun was sinking by the time he returned home, cold and thoughtful. Now he was worried. He tried to recall when he had last seen her, how many days ago it was. When had he last fed or talked to her?

He asked Grandmother but she gave him a very vague reply, her mind taken up with the food that would be needed for the party after the baby's baptism. At last he went to Grandfather again but not without a sense of shame because he felt it was his fault if Neska had disappeared. For a long time he had hardly remembered that she existed.

'What can have happened to her?' he cried anxiously. 'Why doesn't she come when I call her?'

Grandfather didn't know what to say. He, too, was

puzzled. 'She can't have got lost,' he insisted. 'But don't worry. She'll be back.'

He, too, had things on his mind just then and it was easier to console him with a few hopeful words than try to work out what might have happened to her.

Again that night Pablo dreamt he heard a dog barking. At least, he thought it was a dream until, struggling between sleep and wakefulness, he heard the sound again, loud and insistent. It was Neska, he was sure of it, and sleepiness vanished as he jumped out of bed and ran to the window. Carefully, as silently as possible, he opened the window and unlatched the shutters. The yard was in darkness but there was no doubt that Neska was down there.

He called her name in a loud whisper and she answered with a volley of excited barks.

'Ssh!' he exclaimed. 'You'll wake everyone. I'll come down in a minute.'

'What's the matter, Pablo?' his father called from the next room.

He went to the door. 'It's Neska. She's come back. She's barking downstairs.'

'Go back to bed. You'll catch a cold.'

'But she's come back. She's downstairs.'

'All right, but there's no need to wake us all up. If she's come back, she'll still be there in the morning. Now get back to bed. You're going to wake the baby.'

His mother woke up and the whispered explanations began all over again, and then the baby woke up and began to howl.

'Now look what you've done,' she snapped. 'I knew you'd wake her up. Get back to bed and don't let's have any more nonsense. You think too much of that dog.'

Pablo's father lit the oil-lamp on the bedside table. By this time the baby was screaming in spite of everyone's efforts to shush it. Pablo was disconcerted, unable to understand how it could scream so much. It was a terrible, nerve-racking noise.

'She's hungry. I'll have to prepare her a bottle!' exclaimed

Pablo's mother. 'You see what you've done,' she accused him. 'It's going to take ages to warm up some milk, with no electricity or gas. Get back to bed at once, do you hear.'

Blinking back his tears, Pablo did as he was told. It was the first time his mother had shouted at him and he didn't really know why. He met his grandmother on the way, who had got up to see what was the matter with the baby and began to scold him for opening the window and letting in the freezing night air. She closed both shutters and windows with a slam before Pablo even had time to call out to Neska again and bundled him into bed.

The ashes in the brazier were still warm and, after a while, the baby's milk was heated sufficiently and the howls were cut off just as suddenly as they had begun. Grandmother mumbled angrily about modern fads and fancies.

'No wonder the poor thing screams so much, having to wait so long to be fed. She's brought some funny ideas back from

Germany, I must say. And you get to sleep,' she shouted at Pablo, seeing how he watched and listened. 'If you hadn't got out of bed and opened the windows, none of this would have happened.'

For some time Pablo lay awake, his face hidden by the bedclothes, not wanting anyone to know how miserable he felt. Neska didn't bark again and he wondered what she was doing. Had she found shelter in the old kennel, because surely the barn door was shut, or had she curled up under the bottom steps near the kitchen door to wait for morning. He refused to think that she might have gone away again. He was miserable until he started to think about her, forgetting how both his mother and grandmother had scolded him.

Eagerly he ran down to look for her the next morning before going to school but there was no sign that she had been there. He asked his father and grandfather, who had got up before him, if they had seen her but they shook their heads.

'Perhaps you heard another dog, the hunting dog,' suggested his father. 'I don't remember hearing her bark.'

'You were probably dreaming,' Grandfather said. 'I expect you were thinking about her when you fell asleep and that's why you thought you heard her barking.'

'But I saw her, I know I did,' he insisted. 'She was right here in the yard.'

'Well, she isn't here now. Maybe you dreamt that too.'

Grandfather looked down at Pablo seriously. He knew how much Pablo loved his dog and he wondered if worry, and perhaps a sense of guilt, had made him imagine he had seen her. There had been no sign of her for days and it made no sense that she should appear and disappear so quickly in the middle of the night. He himself had begun to believe that they would never see her again, but how could he tell Pablo this? The boy's face was paler than he had ever seen it.

He gripped his shoulder and said comfortingly, 'Don't worry. If she really did come back last night, she'll come back again.'

'But why has she gone away again?' he cried, unable to understand.

Grandfather shrugged. He didn't have an answer ready.

At school, Pablo asked Don Elicio the same question. The teacher knew quite a lot about Neska because whenever he could Pablo talked about her or mentioned her in his essays. Lately, he had been very quiet and distracted in the classroom so that when Don Elicio asked him if anything was wrong he wasn't surprised to hear that it had to do with Neska.

'Tell me about her. When did she disappear? Has she ever gone off before and come back?'

Pablo rushed to answer as well as he could, pouring out most of Neska's history in a few minutes. It was a relief to talk about her and to blame himself for her disappearance.

Don Elicio was thoughtful for a while and then he asked, 'Was she going to have puppies again?'

Pablo stared at him. He hadn't thought of that.

'When did she have the last ones?' Don Elicio asked.

'I don't remember. It was marked on the old calendar but that was thrown away when we got the new one. It was before it snowed, I remember that.'

'Dogs can have puppies about every six months. Do you think it was about six months ago when she had the last ones?'

Pablo thought back, recalling as he did so those tiny bodies and her unhappiness at losing them. He looked at Don Elicio.

'Do you think she's got some more puppies and has hidden them so they can't be taken away again?'

'It's possible. She was very upset the last time, wasn't she? I don't suppose she wants it to happen again.'

An uncontrollable grin spread over Pablo's face as his heart leapt with excitement. Neska with puppies again, and clever enough to hide them so that this time Grandfather couldn't kill them! It was a wonderful thought. He always knew that she was the most intelligent dog alive.

He went dashing home from school that afternoon, filled

with excitement and joy, longing to tell everyone what he knew, longing to find Neska and give her a great bowlful of food. She must be starving and that's why she had come back. He'd tell Grandmother to get something extra prepared for her. There were more leftovers now with his parents at home, and . . .

He stopped because another idea occurred to him, an idea which cut short the happiness that sang inside him, replacing it with a hollow of dread. If Grandfather knew, he would get rid of the puppies again. Even though Neska had hidden them, he would search until he found them. He couldn't have half a dozen dogs roaming round the farm. There was neither room nor food for them. He had made Pablo understand that very clearly the last time and he himself knew that it would be impossible to find homes for them in the village.

So, instead of dashing on home, he stopped and sat down on a stone in the lane, hugging his knees, wondering what to do. He couldn't tell his mother. She didn't even like Neska and his father would probably think the same as everyone else. They were going to leave the farm anyway and they wouldn't be able to take all those puppies to the city with them. The flat was hardly even big enough for Neska.

Where did she have them, anyway? It couldn't be anywhere near the farmhouse. There was nowhere she could hide them sufficiently well for them to remain undiscovered and in the fields themselves there were no hiding places. And hadn't he looked for her everywhere, calling her name?

He stared about, eyebrows thoughtfully sunk. The only hiding place was the forest. There it was almost impossible to see a wild animal, so well did the colours and thickness of the foliage hide them.

He remembered the times he had gone into its depths with Neska and she had bounded ahead, disappearing in a second. Often he could hear her and knew she was nearby but he couldn't see her. He would stand still, straining ears and eyes, waiting for her to return yet hardly daring to call in case some other creature instead of Neska heard him.

Usually she would make him jump as she bounded back to him, appearing suddenly from where there had been only thick bracken or a tangle of fallen boughs. Yes, it was very possible that she had hidden her puppies in the forest where no one, not even he, could find them.

He smiled again as he got to his feet, prepared to go home now and keep the secret. He knew she would come back again, he knew he hadn't dreamt it, and he must have food prepared for her because she wasn't the best of hunters and would be terribly hungry, feeding her younglings with the strength of her own body. But how could he prepare food for her without Grandmother noticing? That was a problem he would somehow have to solve. He knew that, even if it meant stealing from the other dog, he would do it for Neska's sake.

There was one thing of which he was sure. This time no one was going to take the puppies away from her. She had proved her right to them and her devotion by hiding them away even from the eyes of the human she most loved and trusted. She was right not to trust anybody and he would try faithfully not to reveal in any way the secret Don Elicio had helped him discover.

14

Neska came back again the next night. Pablo had already left her bowl of food under the steps, where the smell would lead her to it without it being noticed by Grandmother. The next morning he grinned with satisfaction to find it empty. For two or three days he saw nothing of her. He knew she came because every morning the bowl was empty. Every morning his heart beat a little faster, as he hoped to see her but, at the same time, he was glad she hadn't stayed in case someone else should notice that she was a mother again.

It wasn't as difficult to keep the secret as he had thought it was going to be. With the baby capturing everyone's attention, people were hardly aware that he existed unless he did something that made the baby cry, when everyone fell on him with loud complaints and scoldings. These days, nearly everything he did at home was wrong. He left the door open, he made a lot of noise, he forgot to wash his hands before coming near the baby's cot, once he knocked the feeding bottle on the floor and another time he trod on the dummy. His mother was quite sure that in this primitive house all kinds of infections abounded to attack the new-born child, which made Grandmother very cross, especially since Pablo had been reared there – and he was as healthy as any boy. Everyone was on edge and it seemed to Pablo that he got the blame for everything.

The weather was warming up as spring advanced. There was plenty of rain but also days of sun. Dawn broke sooner and dusk came later. Pablo kept outside as much as possible, preferring to kick about in the barn on wet days rather than be scolded upstairs, and when it was sunny he played in the yard, keeping as far from the baby's pram as possible when it was put out for her to sleep in the fresh air. Hardly anyone asked him what he was doing or where he went. They seemed pleased that he kept out of their way. Even Grandfather didn't need his help with the animals, having stronger arms than his own to do most of the work now.

Perhaps it was because Grandfather had more spare time that he found out about Neska. One morning he said to Pablo, 'That dog of yours has got some puppies somewhere, hasn't she?'

Pablo blushed hotly scarlet far too quickly to be able to deny it. He hung his head and said nothing.

'I suppose they're up in the hills,' he went on.

'You won't kill them, will you?' begged Pablo, his eyes more expressive than any words as he looked up again. 'She hid them on purpose because you killed them last time.'

Grandfather looked at him. He knew he ought to be hard and practical but Pablo was going away from him so soon and he didn't have the heart to deny him anything.

'Please, Grandfather,' he said earnestly, not knowing what he was thinking but realizing that some battle was going on inside him.

The farmer sighed. 'All right,' he said at last and, as Pablo flung his arms round him with a cry of joy, gruffly added, 'But don't steal any more food from my dog. It's not his fault.'

Pablo promised and his heart was lighter now that his secret was shared. The next day Neska actually came back in the early evening. She threw herself on him with crazy delight, licking him all over, hurting him with her claws as she clung to him. Her coat was so thick that it was difficult to tell how thin she was but, as Pablo fondled her, he discovered that she was hardly more than bone. The puppies were eating her up alive. He didn't know how many she had nor how old they were but he knew that for days she had lived on half rations and that each day they would demand more of her.

Grandmother saw him with her and stopped with surprise.

She came to look at her, lying on her flank, panting with exhausted joy, her tongue lolling out.

'She looks hungry,' she said. 'I wonder where she's been. Well, I suppose I'll have to start cooking up more again. You'd better not go upstairs like that,' she warned Pablo, 'or your mother will create.'

Pablo looked at himself, wondering what she meant. He grinned wryly at the mud Neska had left on his sleeves, chest and trousers. She was moulting and her enthusiastic greeting had covered him with hairs as well as mud. The more he tried to brush them off the more they stuck to his jersey.

He ran after Grandmother. 'Can I have some milk for her?' he begged. 'She's awfully hungry.'

'She should have come back sooner,' she snapped, but Pablo hung around her until he wheedled a bowlful of milk. Neska knew what he was up to and trotted up to the kitchen door, head to one side, eyes pleading, until between the two of them Grandmother couldn't hold out any longer.

Pablo watched with satisfaction as she lapped up the lot, licking and licking round the empty bowl and knocking it over with her nose in case a few drops had spilled on the stones.

'She's still hungry. She wants some more,' he demanded.

'Go on with you. She's not getting any more,' and this time she really meant it.

Neska stretched out against the kitchen wall, where the dying sun caught the stones with the last of its warmth, and Pablo slid down beside her, content to stroke her flank and haunches while, with a sigh, she stretched out her head, shut her eyes and dozed. She looked almost as long as he was, perhaps longer, if you included her thick tail, Pablo thought, and he wondered what her puppies would be like. He smiled with happiness. It was so good to have her back again. Perhaps now she would stay a bit longer each day.

His mother came down the steps, carrying some dirty diapers. Neska looked up at the same time as Pablo.

'She's back, is she!' she exclaimed. 'I thought she'd gone for good.'

Her expression suddenly changed, grew darker. Pablo's heart beat faster and his mind raced to discover what he'd done wrong.

'Just look at your clothes,' she cried at him, 'absolutely covered with hair and muck! That's a new jersey you're wearing, too. The work you make for me, and you couldn't care less about it!'

'Leave the boy alone,' snapped Grandmother, rushing to defend him. 'Whoever heard of wearing new clothes around here, anyway. I told you he should have saved that jersey for Sunday.'

'He's got to learn to be clean and if he thinks we're taking that great filthy beast to the flat with us to cover everything with muck and hairs, he can think again.'

The two women went on arguing but Pablo didn't hear them. It was as if his heart had lost all control and was pounding like a thing gone mad. His head swirled and their voices came and went with the pounding of the blood at his temples. His hand gripped Neska's hair as if it were the only solid thing left for him to hold on to.

'. . . airs and graces . . . spoiling the child . . . breaking his heart . . . great brute . . . no idea . . . should never have married you . . . Germany . . . jealous . . . '

Angry, bitter words were flung back and forth over his head as he pressed his back against the sunny wall, clinging to Neska while the world about him exploded. Grandfather came running up and then his father but neither could stop the two women now. All that they had politely tried to harbour up poured out in a flood and when neither could think of another word they both burst into tears and allowed themselves to be led off in different directions. Grandmother went to the kitchen followed anxiously by her husband and Pablo's mother ran up the steps to the living room, his father bounding up behind her. For the moment they had forgotten about him and Neska. His head no longer swirled and his blood no longer pounded, but tears poured down his cheeks too heartfelt to be expressed by sobs.

Neska felt his unhappiness. She stood up and looked at him, gently wagging the tip of her tail, and then she licked his face. Her tongue was so big that one lick covered half of it. Pablo put his arms round her neck. He couldn't utter a sound but just being so close to her consoled him.

They were like this for a little while and then Neska began to get restless. She was remembering her younglings, alone in the forest, and wanted to get back to them. Almost apologetically she backed away from the boy, ducking her head to escape his encircling arms.

'Don't go,' cried Pablo. 'Stay here with me,' but he knew he was being unfair.

She hesitated for a few seconds, looking at him appealingly, glancing towards the forest, her whole body expressing her anxiety to be off. Pablo sprang to his feet, rubbing his wet face on his sleeve, and spitting out a few of Neska's hairs which had got into his mouth.

'I'll go with you!' he cried, desperate to get away from this place of lost tranquillity, unable to bear either his mother's or his grandmother's tears.

Once she had made up her mind to go, Neska moved quickly, crossing the fields at a pace which Pablo found hard to follow. He cried to her to slow down and at first she obeyed him, but as soon as she was within sight of the trees she broke into a beeline lope that heeded nothing and no one. Pablo ran as fast as he could to keep up with her, yelling to her to wait for him, but within seconds she had reached the fringe of trees and, a moment later, disappeared from his sight.

He ran to where he had last seen her, looking from side to side. No bushes moved, he heard no sound, there were no footprints in the earth. He called her name and listened but all he heard was his own panting. Her younglings meant more to her than he did.

He felt terribly alone on the edge of the forest with the darkness gathering quickly all round him. He knew he ought to go back, there was no point in going on, but he dreaded the thought of returning. It was cold now and he shivered. He longed for Neska and wished she hadn't abandoned him here, on the edge of the darkness. He imagined her with her puppies, being welcomed with eager whimperings and hungry mouths and she, with as great an eagerness, curling herself up round them, offering them all she had.

The sense of his own loneliness, torn between the people he loved and unable to give himself to any of them without some kind of betrayal, swelled into a pain so great that it completely crushed him. He crumpled up on the ground beneath the weight of it, digging his fingers into the earth as if somehow his whole being could be covered and protected by it, and at last his voice cried out his defeat in loud, harsh sobs.

Neska heard him. Stretched on her flank with four puppies rhythmically kneading and pulling, giving her a sensation of utter well-being and comfort, the lonely human sound made her prick her ears and open her eyes. For a moment she quivered, recognizing the beloved voice, but then a puppy lost its hold of her dug and whimpered desperately, blindly searching anew, and the anxious whine that escaped her at that moment was for the puppy, not for the boy. She nosed it closer again until it found the dug and she lay back with a sigh of contentment, having shut the boy's cries from her consciousness.

15

Everyone was very quiet in the farmhouse, except the baby who screamed with impatient hunger several times a day, and although no one said anything in front of Pablo he knew what each person was feeling. His mother couldn't wait to get away from there; Grandmother was longing for her to go but, at the same time, dreading it for with her would go the people she loved most in the world; Grandfather felt sorry for her but knew that the only sensible thing was for the young family to settle themselves in their own way as soon as possible; while his father was angry with both his wife and his mother for making things so difficult for them all.

Pablo himself dreaded another explosion and for this reason at least longed, like his mother, for the two families to separate. He hardly dared breathe or move inside the house for fear that some action of his would be the cause of the next outbreak and escaped from them all as much as he could.

Neska was his only consolation. He knew she would come every day and, in order to escape all other thoughts, he spent every free moment thinking of her, wondering about her babies, determined to find them. He hung about the meadows near the forest waiting for her to appear. Sometimes he even carried her food with him so that she wouldn't have to go to the farmhouse for it, and watched with delight as she swallowed it in about five noisy gulps.

It wasn't enough for her. She finished it so quickly, anxiously looking up for more and almost swallowing the bowl in her eagerness not to miss the slightest morsel. Pablo felt her body and it was thinner than ever. Those puppies were growing fast and had appetites as great as her own.

However, when she knew there was no more to eat, she was happy to flop down in the grass beside him, letting him fondle her and talk while she panted and dripped saliva on to his arms.

Pablo couldn't avoid remembering his mother's threat, that Neska couldn't go to the city with them. When she had first uttered it, it had been like the end of the world to him, but since then he had begun to think. He had seen the flat his parents had bought and it wasn't very big, smaller than the farmhouse with only two bedrooms, a living room and a terrace. The kitchen had running water and there was a bathroom with a bath as big as a drinking trough, as well as central heating in every room, but the actual living space was reduced to the minimum needs of a practical modern family. There was no room for Neska to stretch herself out across the floor – there was hardly room for him to do that, either – and if she had to sleep on the terrace at night she would be both uncomfortable and cold. Neska was a farm dog and there was no place for her in the city.

He was sure there was no place for him in the city either, or in that new little flat. He had longed for a baby sister but all Yolanda had brought him so far was trouble. He didn't know that everything had to be so clean and so quiet. He wanted to hold her in his arms and play with her sometimes, but only as a special concession would his mother let him pick her up, hovering about him anxiously all the while and snatching her away almost instantly. Yolanda nearly always began to cry when he held her, the tiny face quite suddenly screwing up into a pained expression, ready for howling. Her cries frightened him because they seemed to drive everyone into a panic.

Grandmother said his mother wasn't used to babies, not disguising her scorn as she spoke, not realizing perhaps that Pablo couldn't bear any criticism of his mother. She told him that it would be far better for him to stay at the farm, at least until his mother had got used to Yolanda. Grandfather overheard her and was cross, telling her not to put ideas into his head. The only person who didn't have much to say was Pablo's father. He spent a lot of time in the city, seeing about a job which was difficult to obtain, and seeing about the flat which was already theirs. He was no more able than anyone else to sort out the problems which their return to the farmhouse had brought and Pablo never even thought of asking for his opinion about Neska. His mother had said that he couldn't take her and he was already sure that on this point at least she would have the last word.

With Neska for company, and as far from the farmhouse and its people as possible, Pablo let his thoughts run on. He had to make a very important decision and he wanted to make it without hurting anybody. He knew he couldn't make everyone happy but he didn't want to make anyone sad.

'It's very difficult,' he told Neska. 'It's all right for you. You've only got one family and you knew what to do right from the beginning. If you had two families, like me, you'd know how difficult it was.'

She wagged her tail and licked his fingers, then she pulled gently at his jersey, wanting to play. She was spending more and more time with him, less and less with the puppies, but the minute something inside her told her she must go to them she left him in a flash, without hesitation. Now she was tranquil and wanted to play, but Pablo wanted to think and hardly noticed her actions. She kept on at him, prancing round him, nipping, eyes bright, tail waving, and at last she began to bark, determined to have her way.

'All right!' he cried. 'I suppose you're right.'

He searched about for a stone and threw it as far as he could, his face lighting up as he watched her dash after it, bounding with all the joy and energy she possessed. When she found it she began to growl and worry it, pushing it with her nose, snatching it up only when Pablo was about to grab it again, defying him to take it from her. This was her favourite game and it ended as it always did, the two of them wrestling on the ground together, rolling over and over each other's bodies, Pablo usually getting some part of himself scratched or nipped, until both would sit back exhausted, with equal expressions of satisfaction, the stone forgotten. She made him forget the important decision he had to make.

'And the puppies? Where are they?' he demanded. 'Why won't you let me see them? I promise not to tell anyone where they are. You don't trust me, do you?'

The soft eyes watched him. She seemed to understand the meaning of everything he said but she wasn't giving him any answer, except to assure him of her devotion. But that day, when she got up to leave him, she looked at him with an expression which definitely invited him to follow her.

At first Pablo didn't believe it. He followed, expecting her to dash off at any moment and abandon him, but she trotted confidently along at his side and, at times, a little way ahead, looking back at him impatiently.

She led him a good way into the forest, though along paths that he already knew because he had trodden them before in her company. They came to the rock where she had almost flung herself at the falcon the previous summer and she waited patiently while he halted there, taking in the view.

He could see the farmhouse, smoke threading up and disappearing in the sunlight; he could see Grandfather ploughing a distant field with the two oxen and his mother in the orchard, hanging out diapers and baby clothes. His father had gone to the city again in his car. From the rock, Pablo could see where the road to the city ran. He couldn't see the road itself but there was a brilliant, moving flash of light which told him of the sun catching on someone's windshield. Neska grew impatient, barking for him to follow her.

Her den was quite nearby, a place where one huge rock rested on another, leaving a gap between the two which formed an angle both deep and high enough for Neska, but which neither rain nor wind could enter. There was soil between the cracks in the ancient stone which gave life to grass and a couple of straggly bushes. It would be difficult to see the cave-like entrance from a distance but easy to discover when close to it.

Pablo caught his breath at the first sight of the four young puppies who craned their necks, aware of their mother's closeness. As she came up to them they began to scrabble towards her. Their eyes were just open – not much use yet, especially with the sun shining directly into them – but their noses and ears told them all they needed to know. Neska gave a short, soft growl as Pablo made to step closer, then she hurried to join them, enduring their combined attack with a resignation born of devotion. The sight made Pablo think of beetles or ants crawling over a discovered body to take whatever sustenance it offered, completely impervious to the victim's feelings. But this was only a momentary impression for he saw the joyful expression in Neska's eyes and understood that her greatest pleasure was in giving them all they demanded.

She growled again softly as he approached but didn't really seem to mind. He couldn't get terribly close because the roof of the rock was too low for him, but he sat by the bushes and watched how they guzzled until one by one their eyes closed, their little jaws lost grip of the dug which slipped free as they slithered to the earth in a semiconscious state of satisfaction, their bellies swollen, their legs and tails stiff. Neska disturbed them all for a while by licking and licking until their cleanliness satisfied her and then she became aware of Pablo again, staring at him as if to say, 'Well, here they are. What do you think of them?'

Two of them were grey with black muzzles, just like her, and the other two must have taken after their sire, with a reddish tone to their coats that just now glistened in the sunlight. Pablo sat and stared at them, completely entranced.

When at last he was tempted to stroke them Neska didn't mind. She uttered another soft growl of warning but let him touch them all, one by one. She growled more fiercely when he tried to pick one up and even began to sit up, so he left it alone and contented himself with just stroking and watching.

'They're beautiful,' he breathed, his eyes shining with love for them all.

They were Neska's, so they were his. She was sharing them with him at last, but she was almost as jealous as his own mother with Yolanda when he wanted to touch them. It must be a feeling common to all mothers, he decided.

The spring sun was warm on the back of his head. He could have sat there all day, just watching Neska and the puppies, forgetting all about time and the problem he still hadn't resolved, but the very tranquility of the place reminded him that the minute he went away he would leave it all behind. With a hand fondling Neska's haunches and sometimes straying to the nearest puppy, he forced his mind back to reality.

His parents were ready to leave the farm. They had bought furniture and, although his father hadn't actually started work in the factory, he expected to do so from one week to another. After the terrible argument between his mother and Grandmother, he couldn't understand why they hadn't already packed their things and left. He couldn't take Neska, firstly because his mother wouldn't have her and, secondly, because she was too much needed here. She couldn't abandon her puppies.

No, she couldn't abandon them and he couldn't abandon her. Who would care about her once he went away? Who would feed her? Grandmother didn't know she had puppies and only put out the usual food for her. He couldn't ask for more food without giving away Neska's secret, so it was up to him to provide what she lacked and what, very soon, the puppies themselves would be needing.

It was easy to think clearly up there in the high part of the forest. All his doubts and heartache fell away. He loved his parents as much as he loved his grandparents and Neska but they didn't need him. They had lived without him for all these years and now they had his baby sister. Neska and his grandparents needed him much more than they did. Without him they would be alone. Without them, he too would be lonely. He wondered how it was that sometimes, even though you loved someone, you could be lonely. He never felt lonely with Neska or with his grandparents. It was only with his parents that he seemed to feel like that, but he didn't know why.

When at last he decided that he had to go back to the farm, the sun had gone and a coldness was creeping over everything. Neska looked up at him but wouldn't desert her puppies. She wagged the tip of her tail as he stood up but that was all she would concede to him just then. He gave her head a last fondling as he said goodbye and then he hurried away, beginning to realize how late it was and that perhaps a scolding would be waiting for him. But at least he went back with a load lifted from his heart. He had made his decision and was no longer torn inside.

His mother was in the orchard, collecting the washing from the line between the trees, as he ran up. She dropped the things on the grass to give him a hug as she cried, 'They've written to your father at last! He can start work on Monday. We're going to move into the flat tomorrow.'

There was such joy in her eyes as she gave him the news that Pablo couldn't doubt her previous unhappiness. There were so many things he didn't understand about adults – so often they seemed to be feeling the opposite of what they actually expressed – but at this moment he knew that his mother was bursting with happiness which she wanted to share with him.

'Come on, Pablo. Help me take these things indoors. There are so many things to be done if we're to make an early start tomorrow.'

She was so happy that she didn't notice his silence. She turned to finish taking the things from the line while he piled the diapers into his arms and walked ahead to the house. Grandmother was at the kitchen door. She said nothing.

She just watched him, but, as Pablo went up the steps, the gaze he couldn't see seemed to make an ache in his back.

How easy it had been up in the hills with Neska to decide to stay at the farm. How difficult it was in reality to reject the flood of happiness with which his mother had greeted him just now! Faith in his decision tottered, his heart beat and his face burned. How could he tell her? Did he want to tell her? Neska, Grandmother . . . The doubt he thought he had tossed off came flooding back. He loved them all. How could he possibly choose?

'Come on, Pablo. You're in a dream!' his mother exclaimed behind him. He hadn't heard her come in. 'Your father will be back soon and he wants us to have the things ready. There won't be room in the car tomorrow for all of us as well as everything else, so he's going to take as much as he can to the flat tonight.'

'So soon?' Pablo managed to scrape out.

His mother at last noticed his state.

'What's the matter?' she asked, concern driving the happiness from her eyes. 'Tell me. What's the matter?'

'I . . . well . . . ' He hadn't the courage to begin.

He knew he must stick by his decision, reached with a clear mind such a short time ago, but he ached to surrender. At that moment surrender was the easiest thing open to him. He suddenly saw that he was wrong about his mother. She did love him. She did need him. She wanted him so much that she hadn't even imagined that he wouldn't go with her.

'Pablo!' she cried, moving towards him with outstretched arms, her eyes wide with anxiety.

He stepped back to escape her embrace, instinctively knowing that with her arms around him he would surrender, and harshly cried out, 'I'm not going with you. I'm staying here. I'm staying here with my grandparents and Neska.'

'Pablo!' cried his mother again. She looked as though she had been hit. 'You don't know what you're saying.'

He nodded fiercely. 'I do. I do, and I'm not going. I want to stay here. I want to stay here.'

He flung himself into her arms and buried his head

against her, his whole being telling her how much he wanted to be with her even as he repeated again and again, 'I want to stay here. I want to stay here.'

Grandmother came in just at that moment. It was a bad moment at which to arrive. Pablo's mother turned on her, still clinging to the boy.

'You've put him up to this. It's your fault. You've been trying to turn him against me all along.'

'You're crazy. I haven't said anything to him. I don't even know what you're on about. What's happened?'

Both of them were immediately hysterical.

'Come to your grandmother,' she pleaded to Pablo. 'Tell me what's the matter. What's happened?'

'Leave him alone!' Pablo's mother gripped him fiercely. 'He's my son and he's coming with me. You've had him long enough. The best years. I want him now and I'm entitled to have him. He's not staying here, no matter what you've put into his head.'

'Ah! So he's said he doesn't want to go with you, eh! Well, that doesn't surprise me. You've done nothing but scold him for weeks. I've said nothing to him. If he doesn't want to go, he knows the reason better than anybody. Tell her, Pablo! Tell her why you don't want to go.'

Pablo struggled out of his mother's arms, desperation tearing him to pieces.

'Leave me alone!' he screamed at both of them as he dashed towards the door. He pulled it open and, looking at both of them with tears streaming down his cheeks, cried, 'I hate both of you, both of you, and I don't want to be with anybody! Leave me alone.'

He flung himself down the steps, almost falling over Grandfather who was hurrying to find out what was happening now. Grandfather tried to grab him but he escaped his arms and fled to the barn where he threw himself down on Neska's bed, crying and crying until there wasn't a tear or a feeling left inside him.

16

The next day Pablo went to live in the city with his parents. The adults had all got together without him to discuss the situation and then they had talked to him. Grandfather had done the explaining. They had all decided that he ought to go with his parents because he belonged with them, but if he wasn't happy and really wanted it he could come back to the farm. They didn't ask him what he thought of this arrangement. They told him what they had arranged. Pablo himself was too exhausted either to care or think. He sat in the car, at the front beside his father, and watched the scenery flash by, everything green with new spring colours, so many greens with flashes of white and yellow and purple of the wild flowers growing everywhere.

In the city Pablo arranged his model air-planes and motor-bikes on the shelves of the new furniture in his room and stuck his school books in the bureau that was just for him – so that he could do his homework properly, without inter-ruptions, his father had said.

He looked after the baby while his mother went shopping. She didn't cry so much now and when she was awake she would smile at him and cling to his finger. Her nails were long and fine. Every day his mother went with Pablo to a different school, talking to caretakers, teachers and, when she was lucky, the headmaster himself. All the schools were full. There was no place for him and there wouldn't be a place until September. They even went to the most expen-sive school in the city, which was a bus-ride away, only to be told the same.

By then two weeks had passed. Pablo's father was happy

at the factory. He worked long hours but he didn't mind. He wanted Pablo to go to the best school. He wanted him to go to university one day. He didn't want him to have to work in a factory to earn a living and he didn't mind how much he worked to get these things for Pablo who, except for weekends, only saw him when they had supper together before bedtime.

Pablo watched television every day because he had nothing else to do. It fascinated him because he had hardly ever watched it before. There was a television in the tavern in the village, where everyone went on Sunday nights to watch the football matches, but they lived a long way from the village and didn't go to the tavern very often. Pablo sometimes used to go with Grandfather on Sunday mornings, to watch the men play draughts or dominoes, but there was nothing on television on Sunday mornings.

The flat was on a busy street and there was nowhere for Pablo to play except on the pavement which was dangerous. So he stood on the terrace and looked down at the traffic and passers-by. It was an interesting occupation, too. He had never seen so many people, all unknown, in his life. He knew everyone in the village. Here he didn't even know the people who lived next door.

When his mother let him go down to the street he tried to find the shop he had visited with Grandfather, where they had bought the collar for Neska. He couldn't find the shop and he couldn't find his way back home. He had to ask and ask and this was an ordeal for him because it wasn't easy to halt a rushing stranger who seemed to have such a lot on his mind. More often than not they didn't know where his street was, anyway. For a while fear struck him as he wondered if he'd got the name wrong. He imagined never finding it again. He imagined wandering up and down the grey streets, one so much like another, until he dropped with exhaustion. No one would care and his mother would think he had run away from her.

In the middle of his fear he discovered a place he knew. It was the cathedral. He pushed open the inner door and timidly stepped inside. At once all the noise from the street disappeared and he almost felt happy as he recognized those tall columns which had reminded him of the trees in the forest. He forgot that he was lost. His feet ached so much that he decided to sit down on one of the benches. He dipped his fingers in the stone bowl of holy water and made the sign of the cross on his forehead, remembering how he had done this the last time with Grandfather, and sank gratefully on to a bench.

It was intensely quiet in the cathedral, quiet and cold. There was hardly anybody there – an old woman lighting a candle where dozens already burned steadily in front of an altar, shuffling with slippered feet to a bench just ahead of him where she knelt down to pray; and a couple of tourists who wandered round looking at everything, straining their necks as he had done the first time, and talking in whispers.

He began to remember that day with Grandfather, how it had rained, the lovely meal they had had, the bus ride with the collar smelling so new in his hands, and his thoughts wandered on to Neska.

What would she be doing now? Did she have enough to eat? Did Grandfather look after her? Would he keep his promise about the puppies? They were the same thoughts that assailed him every night when he got into bed and his mother switched the light out. Neska and his grandparents were constantly in his thoughts before he fell asleep, but Neska most of all because she had depended on him and he had failed her. He wondered if she would find food for her puppies. Would she learn to hunt for them? She was such a bad hunter. Her instinct was to guard and protect, not to hunt. How different from Grandfather's hunting dog whose nose was sensitive to every smell and whose body registered even the direction of the scent he followed. Neska would be almost sitting on a rabbit before she smelt it. He smiled to himself at her clumsiness but it worried him. How would she find food in the forest?

He felt comfortable in the cathedral and his thoughts wandered on to his parents. He wondered how soon they

would take him to visit the farm but he dared not ask his
mother in case she should think it was because he wasn't
happy with her. And he was happy, he really was. There
was no more tension. He was getting to know his parents
better. His baby sister was beginning to notice him and
cry less when he touched her.

His father had taken him for a walk in the park one
Sunday. They had talked about all sorts of things – that was
when his father had told him how he must study hard to go
to university one day and not be like him who had stopped
going to school when he was twelve because Grandfather
had needed him on the farm. He talked about Germany,
which was a wonderful place but not like home; he talked
about the factory, which was a mysterious world for Pablo;
and he tried to explain why they couldn't all be happy
together at the farm. He said that when two women loved
the same man they were always jealous and suspicious of
each other, even though one was a mother and the other a
wife. Nature had made them like that and there was nothing
that anyone could do except keep them apart. All that his
father said seemed very sensible to Pablo. Most of all he
enjoyed being talked to as if he were grown up. Grandfather
always treated him like a child.

Thinking it over, Pablo knew that if it hadn't been for
his worry about Neska he would have been happy. There
were a lot of things he missed but there were a lot of new
things to attract his attention. If only he had a school to go
to or some friends to play with, the hours wouldn't
seem so long. If only he had Neska everything would be
perfect.

Just then he noticed someone he recognized in the shadows
of the cathedral. The face was strange but at least the clothes
were familiar. It was a priest. Here at least was someone
Pablo could talk to, someone who would stop and listen
and who might be able to tell him how to get home. The
priest was indeed as friendly as Pablo had hoped. He listened
and asked questions and learnt almost the whole of Pablo's
life history in a very short while. Eventually he took him

back to his flat by car and even went upstairs with him to talk to his mother. He told Pablo that he could come and see him any time he wanted to and this made him happy because at last he knew someone in the city who had time to stop and listen to him.

When Pablo's father realized that it was impossible to find a school for his son he was very worried. Pablo had to pass the summer exam or he wouldn't be able to go on with next year's studies. He would have to repeat the whole year again, which was a waste of time as well as a waste of money.

'I'm going to talk to Don Elicio,' he decided one night after supper. 'After all, he still has his place in the school there.'

'But then he won't be able to live with us. He'll have to go back to your parents,' his wife protested.

'He could spend the weeks with them and the weekends with us. It would be better than having him lose a whole term of school and not pass the exams in June.'

Pablo's mother took a lot of convincing. She didn't want to give up her son, not even for a day. She was certain that his grandmother would try to influence him against her and, although she didn't say this aloud, both Pablo and his father knew what she was thinking. As for Pablo himself, when his father talked about sending him back to the village his heart leaped for joy. He could be with Neska again and make sure she was getting enough to eat. He could be sure that Grandfather would keep his promise about the puppies. The very look in his eyes, although neither parent knew the reason for it, convinced them that he ought to go back and finish the school year with Don Elicio.

So it was that the very next weekend Pablo found himself once again with his grandparents. Grandmother cried with joy when she learned he was to stay with them till the summer and immediately rushed off to prepare his bed. Pablo's father explained to Grandfather the reason for their decision, and said that instead of returning home every weekend as they had originally thought – which was impractical because of the distance – they would fetch him whenever the weekend was stretched to include a holiday, which would give him three or four days with his parents instead of only one night.

Grandmother managed to prepare quite a feast in spite of the unexpectedness of their arrival and while they ate they chatted about neutral things. Pablo's father asked about the work, Grandfather talked about a plan he had for rearing beef cattle, the two women talked about the baby while Yolanda herself slept right through the meal which was very obliging of her. Grandfather mentioned that there had been a plague of foxes, more numerous that year than for many he could remember, and that he'd had to rewire the chicken pen to keep them out. A number of chickens and rabbits had been stolen from different farms and half a dozen foxes had been trapped.

'There's still a few of them hanging around,' he went on, and looked at Pablo. 'We're missing that Neska. If she was here, she'd frighten them all off.'

'Haven't you seen her?' His voice was anxious. He had hoped to see her as soon as they arrived at the farm but, on not being able to find her, assumed that she was with her younglings.

'Not for several days. She was here . . . when was it? I remember feeding her myself, not more than four days ago, but she hasn't been back since then.'

'Huh!' grunted Grandmother. 'I told you to tie her up last time she came back. With everybody so jumpy about the foxes it's not good to have a dog roaming around. She never used to roam. She's been getting some bad habits lately. You'd better go and look for her, Pablo, and tie her up in the barn when you find her.'

He nodded. Suddenly what was left of his appetite disappeared. If Neska hadn't been back for four days what had she been living on? He longed to go and look for her but couldn't run off until his parents had left.

Luckily, they didn't stay long that afternoon. They didn't want to get home too late. His mother hugged him very fiercely and promised they would be thinking about him all the time and come to see him just as often as they could, and his father told him to study hard and get good marks in the exams.

'You must make up for lost time,' he reminded him.

Then they were off, with Yolanda in her car seat in the back of the car. Pablo waved until they were out of sight, too anxious about Neska to feel sorry about their going.

'I'm going to look for Neska,' he told Grandfather immediately afterwards.

'It's a good idea. But what about those puppies? I suppose you know where they are?'

He said yes somewhat unwillingly, affected by the way Grandfather looked at him.

'You know she can't keep them,' he went on.

'Why not? They're not doing any harm.'

'Not now they aren't, but what about when they get older? What are they going to live on? You'd better bring them down to the farm and let me get rid of them.'

'But, Grandfather, you promised – '

'I promised because I knew you were going away,' he interrupted, angry with himself. 'I thought you wouldn't know. Pablo, you must understand. We don't live in a world of dreams. Those puppies are going to be dogs one day and they're going to be hungry. They've got to eat, the same as we have to, and they're going to look for their food in the easiest possible way. Do you understand?'

Pablo nodded miserably. He understood only too well. Neska was destined never to have puppies because when men and nature differed in opinion, men usually won. They always had excellent reasons for destroying what was inconvenient to them. They never used their hearts, only their heads, which were more like machines every day. He couldn't say all these things to Grandfather but they were expressed in his eyes, scornfully and bitterly.

Grandfather squeezed his shoulders. 'In some ways I've let you down, haven't I, Pablo? I've not always told you the truth. I've wanted to make things easy for you – or easy for myself, perhaps. But nothing's easy, Pablo. Nothing's easy. You'll find that out for yourself, bit by bit.'

There wasn't anything else to say. After a silence Grandfather suggested, 'I'll find you a sack. It might be easier to carry them like that,' and he hurried off to the barn to look for one.'

17

The cows were out in the fields. They looked at Pablo as he passed them, jaws moving, tails swishing, and forgot him as they dropped their heads for the next mouthful of grass. The ground was soggy with the recent rain and the new shoes Pablo was wearing were thick with mud. He kept slipping because they didn't cling to the earth like his old boots did and soon dampness was seeping through them to his socks. He didn't notice the discomfort, any more than he noticed the cows, his mixed thoughts and emotions demanding all his attention. Sometimes he had to bite his lip to hold back the indignation at the knowledge of his own helplessness.

Grandfather was wrong in so many things but in this Pablo had to accept that he was right. Perhaps Neska wouldn't mind so much, now that she would have his company again. But what about the next time and the time after? Don Elicio had told him that dogs had puppies twice a year. Was Grandfather going to kill them every time? Why did they have to be born? If he was there to look after her he would make sure she never had the opportunity again, but if he wasn't there who would care about her? Grandfather would chain her up, Grandmother would feed her, and both would forget about her after that.

She mustn't be chained, she mustn't, but what was the use of making Grandfather promise? He didn't know the real meaning of a promise, or at least he didn't understand what a promise meant to him. He told him whatever he wanted to hear. He made promises easily because he wouldn't keep them if it wasn't convenient, and then he made excuses and expected them to be accepted.

Pablo kicked the ground savagely as he trudged beneath the trees, wondering why it was that grown-ups always had explanations for everything, for all the mistakes they made and all the promises they broke. Sometimes he hated Grandfather for making him believe so many things that weren't true and then expecting him to understand reality. It wasn't fair to him. Truth might be hard but disillusion was cruel, and with these thoughts Pablo almost dreaded finding Neska again because he was deceiving her, too.

One day he would leave her again, break faith with her, and nothing he could say or do would stop her from succumbing to the fate that had awaited her almost from birth – confinement at the end of a chain. He had made her believe that life was chasing across the fields, fighting and playing with him, attacking shadows and sticks and bringing him stones. It was all she knew, all he had taught her. He had even made her believe that she had the right to become a mother and nurse her puppies, that she had a right of her own to live.

All of it was a lie. She was alive because Grandfather had saved her for him, and she was free because he had begged for her and his grandparents couldn't refuse him anything. So he was as bad as Grandfather, ignoring reality to give himself happiness, discovering now that one day reality caught up with dreams and smashed them. He saw clearly now that he was as guilty as Grandfather and he began to understand, just a little, what he had meant with his words.

Nothing was easy.

He reached the rock which towered above the tops of the trees below. Neska's den wasn't far away now and, in spite of his mission, he couldn't prevent a leap of excitement in his heart. If he called, she would surely come bounding to answer him. The memory of her hefty, enthusiastic greetings made him smile. Then he wondered if she would let him take the puppies. The last time she had growled at him when he'd tried to pick one up. How right she was not to trust him!

'Neska! Neska!'

The drawn-out sounds penetrated the silence and disappeared. Pablo waited, listening, expecting to hear an answering bark. He became aware of birds and, from far off, a melodious human voice. He looked for its owner and saw on one of the dark green slopes a farmer reaping the tall spring grass. His strokes were neat and rhythmic and all about him was an empty patch which he had already cut. He sang as he reaped, unaware of being watched from so far away. Pablo couldn't make out the words but the sound was cheering. A little donkey stood not far away, his back already laden with a mound of grass.

Neska didn't come and so Pablo set off on the last lap of his climb, sure he would find her feeding the puppies and therefore unwilling to abandon them. But when he reached the den, Neska wasn't there. The puppies were alone and they shrank back at the sight of him, suspicious and fearful. They flattened their ears and showed their teeth, their growls sufficiently ferocious to stay the hand he had instinctively stretched out towards them.

How they had grown! They had doubled in size, but there was something about their appearance that puzzled Pablo. Three weeks ago they had been all fat and fur, soft to the touch and self-contented. Now they were gaunt and dirty-looking, with none of the innocent, playful expression he had expected. He realized that they were hungry, desperately hungry.

He had brought some food in a newspaper for Neska and wondered if these small creatures would be able to eat it. There were a lot of chicken bones among the mess of beans and rice but even as he doubtfully spread the paper on the ground, the little animals struggled to all fours and, forgetting fear and suspicion, ravenously fell on the contents. They fought with each other, trod over it, even fell in it before each one seriously settled down to devouring all he could and, as Pablo had guessed, they weren't very good at it. He remembered Neska's first efforts at eating solid food and what a mess she'd made of it.

Very soon their noses and eyes were all stuck up, but they

struggled on, growling ferociously all the while, and Pablo saw that they swayed and fell over very frequently and made quite hard work of getting up again. In fact, they were on the point of starvation.

So, where was Neska? Why had she abandoned them? Surely they wouldn't be in this state if she was still looking after them.

He called her again, this time cupping his hands round his mouth to make the sound carry farther, but by the time the puppies had eaten as much as they could hold and each one was chewing at a chicken bone, there was still neither sign nor sound of her.

Something had happened to her and Pablo felt sick with fear when at last he accepted this. He remembered Grandfather talking about the foxes and how the farmers had been shooting them. Had they shot her too? Had she gone to steal chickens and been caught? No, that wasn't possible. Grandfather would have known about it.

When had he last seen her? Four days ago, he'd said. It looked as though the puppies hadn't seen her in all that time, either. Perhaps someone had found and kept her. She was a dog worth having, after all. She couldn't have been attacked by another animal – she was far too big and strong. Besides she had that collar to protect her throat.

Could she be sick? No, she would have dragged herself back to the puppies. She wouldn't abandon them. Could she have got caught in a trap? He knew the farmers set traps for foxes and rabbits. But surely she would have answered his call? One bark, however hurt she was.

He would have to look for her. She couldn't be very far away. Where did she go to, except the farm? His heart pounded. It was his fault if anything had happened to her.

He looked at the puppies. They were happier now. One of them was even trying to play, pawing at his companions and shaking his head with a friendly growl. He looked just like Neska, grey and big-boned, with giant paws. The others were a reddish colour, with grey beneath. It was surprising how much energy they had recovered in so short a time.

One of them was tugging at the sack which Pablo had left nearby, reminding him of what he had come for.

He would go and look for Neska first. After he had found her he would come back for the puppies. Let them be happy for a little while longer.

The biggest puppy, the one that looked like Neska, came to sniff at him, gingerly stretching forward, ready to dash away at the slightest provocation. Pablo didn't move. He let the puppy sniff to his satisfaction, longing to pull him into his arms, but not daring to let himself feel for him. Wasn't he going to take him back in the sack for Grandfather to kill?

He pushed all the puppies back into their nest, feeling that they would be safer there. This time they didn't growl at him or flatten their ears. Filling their bellies had made them sleepy and all but the biggest were content to stay where he put them; he had to push him three times before at last he flopped down among the others who were already half asleep.

The afternoon was nearly over. Soon it would be growing dark and Pablo knew that Grandfather expected him home very soon. Besides, he would never find Neska in the shadows and was also half afraid of losing himself once darkness fell. He could tarry no longer if he really wanted to know what had become of his dog.

He went back to the rock which gave him such a good view over the valley and part of the forest and gazed from one side to the other, both near and far. The farmer had gone from the hill and only the lighter-coloured patch told that he had been there. Grandfather was in the field, rounding up the cows. It was probably time to milk them. He wondered if Grandfather would be able to see him. His attention was caught by a flock of crows that flapped and squabbled and plunged between the trees. For several seconds he just watched them, wondering what they were quarrelling about, and then he remembered what Grandfather had once told him – that they were scavengers, keeping the countryside clean by eating up decaying bodies and attacking weaklings. They never attacked anything that was strong. Only the sick and the dead came into their clutches.

Pablo involuntarily shuddered and then he broke into a run in their direction. He had to know what they were fighting over, if only to satisfy himself that it wasn't Neska.

It took him about fifteen minutes to find them again, following animal runs through the thickets and fallen branches. The ground was soft under his feet, soggy with rotting leaves, and the foliage above his head was so thick that he couldn't even see the rock he had left behind to check his bearings. Still he told himself that Neska might be hunting, learning the slow, hard way that only hunger teaches. Perhaps she hadn't heard him. Perhaps she was locked up somewhere. He refused to let his mind dwell on any other possibility as he hurried along, as if just by willing it he could save her from anything worse.

He almost fell over a dead crow. Its wings were spread out and its beak was open.

'Serve you right,' he spat at it with a feeling of repugnance. Grandfather said they were necessary but that didn't mean to say you had to like them.

Before going much further he came across two more. This seemed rather strange to him. What could have caused their deaths? But he didn't stop to wonder for more than a moment. He was near the place he was searching for and time was growing so short.

A couple of crows flew up into the branches with loud cries of warning to their companions who, in their turn, flapped their wings and cried in answer. The forest echoed as they scolded the hasty intruder from a high place in the trees. Then Pablo stopped, suddenly deaf to their cries, for just ahead of him, only a few strides away, lay Neska, or what the crows had left of her, for they had already begun their work.

At that moment Pablo seemed turned to stone. He could neither move forward nor run away, but his eyes could still see, could still register what remained of his beautiful Neska

who lay stretched out in the shadows, her jaws wide apart in the harshest of grins.

Slowly, feeling returned and although he knew he had found her too late he had to go close to be sure. A wave of dizziness hit him in his head and stomach as he looked down on her, hardly able to believe that this brittle, gaping, eyeless thing had been his Neska. What had killed her he could not tell. Surely sickness would not have struck her down so quickly, probably on the way back to her younglings? Perhaps a farmer had shot at her and she had died up here of her wounds.

He could not touch her, not even with his foot. His face twisted with sick agony, he backed away, saying inside himself, 'Neska, Neska, Neska.'

He didn't want the crows to get at her again and with feverish anger began pulling at bracken and broken branches, laying them across her, unaware of the harsh sobs that escaped him as he worked. He gathered up armfuls and arm-fuls of leaves, first covering the mutilated head with the once beautiful white teeth so strangely discoloured, unaware of the fast fading daylight, so full of darkness was his heart. It seemed as though there weren't enough leaves or branches in all of the forest to cover her, and he dragged savagely at ferns and small bushes, trying to tear them from the earth. Bits of them broke off in his hands but the roots resisted. At last, however, the big grey body was buried, perhaps only lightly, but enough to satisfy the boy.

When at last he stopped he realized how tired he was, hot, dirty, his hands stinging with cuts and scratches and growing stiff from their toil. The spot where Neska lay was just another dark place in the forest, a jumble of leaves, old and new, branches and plants intermingled, like everything else in that place. Pablo stood looking at it a little while longer, not thinking now of how he had found her, but of how she had always been – ever ready for a game, ever patient of his whims.

'At least, Grandfather won't be able to chain you up,' he

said. 'You managed to escape that, anyway.' It was his only comfort.

When at last he got back to the farmhouse his grandparents exclaimed at his state. They had started to worry because he had never been out so late before on his own and when Grandmother saw his tear-streaked face and torn and dirty clothes, she cried out with alarm. Grandfather gripped his arm.

'What's happened? Did you find her?'

Pablo nodded, biting his lip. Grandfather's words brought fresh tears to his eyes but, as long as he didn't speak, he could hold them back.

'You don't need to tell me,' he said. 'I can guess. And what about the puppies?'

Pablo started. He had forgotten all about them. What did it matter, anyway? Grandfather was only going to kill them.

'They're dead. Dead,' he cried, struggling free and dashing away from both of them. They would make him talk and just then he couldn't bear it.

He threw himself down on his old bed, for now that his parents had gone the room was his again, and pulled the big pillow over his head. It was cold and fresh and comforting. His head was hot and ached so much.

Grandmother was about to open the door and go in but he heard Grandfather tell her not to. They went away. For a while he heard them talking softly, their voices muffled through the pillow, and then he fell asleep. Later Grandmother came quietly back and covered him with the eiderdown after carefully removing his shoes, but he didn't awake until the next morning; he didn't even dream.

18

The next morning Pablo had to go to school. Grandfather walked down to the village with him because Don Elicio would have to be informed about the new situation. On the way he tried to get the boy to talk about Neska, perhaps because he felt some guilt in the matter. He hadn't done his duty by her but he couldn't actually express this in words, except by showing concern when it was too late. Pablo explained how he had found her and also the dead crows and Grandfather exclaimed with a very strong swear word.

'They've poisoned her,' he cried. 'It's the only explanation, and God knows how many other animals they'll have poisoned at the same time. It's against the law but they don't care.'

'Who, Grandfather? Who?'

'Who but the farmers who've been plagued with foxes? I heard a rumour about it the other week but I didn't take much notice. They bait chunks of meat with strychnine and spread it wherever the fancy takes them. There used to be eagles on this side of the forest once upon a time, not long before you were born, and they were all killed off by baited meat. But not the foxes. They're too clever to be caught like that. They're more likely to die by feeding on the dead crows.' He sighed and shook his head.

'Neska was hungry so she ate the meat she found in the forest,' said Pablo. Then, after a pause, 'Why are people so bad, Grandfather? If it's against the law, why do they do it?'

'It's a war, Pablo, man against nature, nature against man and, like all wars, the ones that have got nothing to do with it usually get destroyed. The eagles and the foxes kept down the rabbits. They never attacked any farm stock. Then all the rabbits fell sick with a man-made plague and there was nothing for the foxes to eat so they started to attack the farms. The farmers used traps and guns and poison against them. They killed off a good many but they also killed the eagles and vultures and a few other animals that probably rotted in the forest without our noticing. I haven't seen a wild cat for years! The rabbits are coming back and so are the foxes, but the eagles have gone for good.'

He sighed again, remembering. 'They were a sight to see, those eagles.'

'They've no right, no right,' protested Pablo, hardly able to keep the tears from his eyes.

His whole body shivered with indignation and he ached with his own helplessness against such barbaric indifference. Nobody really cared about the creatures that died in agony out of their sight, most people didn't even know about them. He would never have known if it hadn't been for Neska and, even though it was against the law, nobody would ever be brought to justice because there was no justice for rabbits or eagles or hungry dogs.

Grandfather put an arm round his shoulders.

'You just have to accept it,' he tried to comfort him. 'You did your best for her.'

'I don't want to accept it!'

All that Grandfather had said burned inside him, making him feel hot even while he shivered. Nobody cared enough to do anything about it, not even Grandfather who sighed over the lost eagles, but he would care, he wouldn't accept it. If he had to fight the whole world, he couldn't just accept that these things happened.

They said nothing else to each other. Grandfather didn't know how to comfort the boy and Pablo's heart and mind were too incensed for words. Last night he had been torn with sorrow but now something much deeper than sorrow moved him. A voice cried out in his head, reiterating with childish futility, 'It's not fair, it's not fair.' Had he still felt like a child he would have cried the words aloud, but childhood had been left behind, perhaps buried beneath the leaves with Neska, destroyed by the same poison.

His return to the classroom caused some comment but eventually Don Elicio restored order and got them working at their different tasks. More than once he realized that Pablo wasn't concentrating, wasn't even listening to him, but every time he looked at him he remembered the farmer's parting words – 'They've poisoned his dog' – and left him alone. He knew what Pablo had felt for Neska and shared the boy's sense of futility. There was no kind of comfort for things like that.

It was a grey day, as grey as Pablo's heart. Through the window he could see wet cobbles and damp walls and, everywhere, grass, moss and dandelions dark with moisture, intensely green against the drab daylight. Although it wasn't raining, everything was wet and the backs of passing oxen steamed. Pablo wondered if Grandmother would let him go into the forest on such a day, when surely daylight would be gone long before night had come, and even while he wondered his heart felt hard. He would go, whether she let him or not. If he had declared to himself his own private war, now was no time to care what Grandmother might say.

Neska's puppies had to be kept alive, if only to atone in some way for the eagles and rabbits and Neska herself. It wasn't a thing he reasoned. They weren't words in his head. It was something he felt in response to everyone's indifference. Someone had to care, someone had to fight. He would defy them all because it wasn't right that they should always win. Something in the forest had to survive.

Pablo did his best. He visited the pups as often as he could. He bought bread in the village for them and stole milk from the cows in the field. He took Neska's bowl for them – the one from Germany with her name on it – and fought them off until he had crumbled the bread and milk into the right consistency. He brought them all the cheese rinds and scraps from the table. He learnt how to clean the rabbits and chickens that Grandmother killed for their meals and she never knew that the yards of useless intestines disappeared into the rapacious guts of Neska's puppies.

Sometimes it seemed to her that the hens were laying less eggs, and she could have sworn that there were less sausages than usual hanging in the fireplace, and as for the biscuits – well, she just couldn't understand how Pablo could eat so many and still have room for supper. His good appetite pleased her immensely; it was surely all the fresh air – he spent so much time out of doors – and she smiled to herself when she thought of the half-loaf she prepared for him with a thick chunk of cheese or a couple of sausages, when he would come home ravenously asking for supper.

In spite of his efforts Pablo couldn't keep all the puppies alive. The first one died only a couple of days after he began to bring them food. She was obviously the weakest and succour had come too late to have any effect on her. There was no doubt that the strongest ate the most for, try as he would to share the food out equally, the big male puppy and the biggest of the bitches always managed to get the most. Pablo couldn't decide why the second one died. She was just dead one day when he got there, at some distance from the nest, and the remaining two trod over her quite carelessly, already fighting each other for what he had brought.

These two showed every intention of clinging joyously to existence, the male puppy looking just like Neska, except

for his pricked ears, the bitch slightly smaller, with the same ears but different colouring.

For a while Pablo had toyed with the idea of taking the remaining pups back to the farm, thinking he might be able to persuade his parents to let him have the male dog in the city, leaving the bitch with Grandfather. The idea of having a new puppy so much like Neska made him forget all his horror of the other one being chained, but when his parents came to visit him one weekend and he mentioned the matter in a roundabout way, his mother was adamant. She said he could have a canary if he wanted to, because they sang very nicely, but that was all. So he kept the puppies secret and fed them when he could and saw how they grew, almost from day to day. They greeted him exuberantly and, when the business of eating was over, included him in their games of chewing and nipping and chasing about. Pablo couldn't visit them daily but he usually managed to get to them at least three times a week, depending on the weather and the homework he was given.

A problem arose when they wanted to follow him home. At first they were quite content to curl up in their nest and sleep off the heaviness of their stomachs, but as they grew bigger they needed less sleep and couldn't understand why they mustn't follow him when he went away. Pablo used to try to wait until they fell asleep but the time would go by and they'd be as lively as ever so that there was no way of leaving them without their noticing. He couldn't tie them up. He couldn't deceive them. He would think he had got away but, all of a sudden, they would be there, yapping at his heels and he would have to take them all the way back.

For their own sakes he had to teach them not to follow him but they were pig-headed little creatures who refused to take his admonitions seriously. How could they understand that they mustn't follow him? He was like mother and brother to them and all their trust was in him. In the end he had to hurt them to make them understand. He found a stick and every time they disobeyed his command to stay, tumbling down the hillside after him, he hit them sharply on their noses, which made them blink and yelp and shake their heads in hurt surprise.

Even like this they didn't want to learn. He had to hit them harder each time. The bitch was more inclined to give in. She would sit back on her haunches and rub her smarting nose with her paws, whimpering dolefully, but the male puppy defied him. He kept out of reach of the stick, halting whenever Pablo halted, head cocked to one side, eyes brightly challenging. When the boy went after him he ran away, tail between legs, dodging beneath bushes and branches to escape punishment, but as soon as Pablo gave up the pursuit he was behind him again, determined to get his way.

At first, Pablo had to force himself to punish him, reminding himself that it was for the puppy's own sake, but after a while the animal's stubborn disobedience filled him with exasperation. He would be late home, Grandmother would start asking questions, one day the puppy would be seen. With these fears pressing him, he would lash out furiously at the puppy, as often as not missing him, and even though the dog sensed his anger he wouldn't be warned by it.

One day, however, he didn't dodge in time and Pablo's lashing stick caught him right across the eyes. The pain must have been acute to judge by the torrent of yelps it produced as he fled blindly away. Pablo wanted to run after him and hold him in his arms, torn by those pain-filled cries, but he knew he mustn't. He hadn't meant to hurt him so much but it was done and perhaps he would learn. He threw the stick down and dashed away, trying to ignore the yelps which seemed never-ending, wishing in his heart that he had never made the puppies need him.

He went back the next day determined to be less friendly with them. They had to learn to be independent of him. They had each other, they weren't alone, they must never come to love him as Neska had done, any more than he must love them. They must learn to live in the hills, to be afraid of man, to look only to the forest for shelter and food. If he couldn't teach them this he might just as well let Grandfather kill them quickly. If he cared about them, he had to be hard, as hard as nature was, as hard as a man. They must never look to him with love unless he was prepared to make slaves of them. If they wanted to be free they had to be alone.

With these thoughts he returned to them, determined from now on only to toss the food to them from a distance and then go away; they always cared more about the food than about him, anyway. They couldn't avoid coming under his dominion if they always looked to him as food-bringer and playmate, and if they were under his dominion he knew that one day, however unwillingly, he would betray them.

It wasn't easy to make this decision for he cared about them in spite of himself. The male puppy reminded him constantly of Neska in looks. He was so bold and defiant and yet so small that Pablo's heart went out to him. As for the bitch, although she wasn't like Neska in looks, she had many of her gentle ways. Even in her games she wasn't as rough as her brother and she had a way of looking at him that was Neska's through and through. Between the two of them they combined all that had been his dog and he couldn't help but love them for all that he tried to harden his heart.

They were basking in the sun when he came upon them, drowsy, hardly aware of him. The male puppy's eyes were swollen and half blinded. He must have been rubbing them a lot because all his head was dirty. But Pablo resisted the urge to tend him. He would get better and, if he'd learned his lesson, it was worth it.

The two animals saw him and ran towards him, the male shaking his head. They almost tore the food from his hands and while they devoured it he went away. He didn't have much spare time that day, anyway, and the sooner he made the break from them the better it would be.

The male puppy saw him leave. He made to follow and then stopped. There was obviously a struggle going on inside him. Pablo turned away, setting off for home. He mustn't look back although every instinct was to do so. The puppy didn't follow and when Pablo took one quick glance, he saw both of them chewing ravenously at the pile of rabbit guts he had thrown to them.

19

Weeks went by. Most Sundays Pablo's parents came from the city to spend the day at the farm and occasionally Pablo spent a long weekend with them at the flat. Now that they no longer lived together, the adults got on surprisingly well. There were no more quarrels, much to Pablo's relief, and Grandmother and his mother talked about Yolanda for hours. Grandmother spent most of the day with the baby in her arms and when once Pablo's mother suggested that such proceedings were going to spoil her, he saw how his father discreetly told her to be quiet. He smiled to himself, remembering what his father had told him in the park, and tried to be particularly nice to his mother to make her forget any annoyance she might feel.

The baby didn't grow as quickly as the puppies but each time he saw her it seemed that she was more aware of everything. She smiled at Pablo, and moved her mouth as if to make words when he talked to her. His mother insisted that she made all sorts of words already but only Grandmother believed her. She made lots of bubbles which afterwards dribbled down her chin and she could bite very hard even though she hadn't any teeth, as Pablo discovered when he let her stick his finger in her mouth. She was like the puppies in that respect. She wanted to eat everything, no matter what it was.

Grandfather mentioned to Pablo's parents the time he spent in the forest. If he had wondered at first about this he had satisfied himself since that it was for no other reason than that he liked to be there. Pablo had promised him that the puppies were dead. He had gone to the forest himself on several occasions with his hunting dog, discovering Neska's burial place but no sign of the puppies. He soon forgot about them. Pablo said he liked to watch the birds and forest animals and Don Elicio had lent him a book about the creatures he might find in the forest.

When Pablo's father heard all this he brought him a pair of army field-glasses which he had bought in Germany. Their lenses were so strong that he could see things at an incredible distance as if they were under his nose, while the closer things were magnified so many times that he saw details never before imagined. Sometimes he couldn't recognize the things he saw because they were so close but, after hours of practice, he became quite skillful with them.

He discovered where the squirrels hid their nuts. He watched birds feeding their young. One day he saw how a baby cuckoo tossed its foster brothers from the nest, a helpless but fascinated spectator of their desperate struggle before they fell. How that monstrous bird stretched itself out and made itself comfortable before the unwitting parents returned! In the forest only the toughest and most determined survived.

With the binoculars he could count the speckles on the backs of a family of baby boars, trotting through a glade at a distance beyond the reach of the naked eye. He saw a roe deer give birth, watching the calf take its first staggering steps and its first bellyful of milk. He saw a pine marten sunning itself on a high oak branch, so much a part of the dappled shadows that it was almost invisible. Rabbits in plenty ventured out with the lengthening shadows, constantly alert, constantly afraid, and there were butterflies, spiders and insects of every kind which he had never noticed before.

He never saw any bears and supposed they had disappeared like the eagles, but one day he made a discovery which caused him to tremble with excitement. There was a family of wolves, far away and high up, where the trees began to thin out towards the barren rock. They were as grey as the rocks among which they hunted, for hunting they were surely engaged upon although it seemed to Pablo that there could be nothing up there for them to eat. They dug up stones and nosed in cracks and, by their actions, he could tell that they discovered something.

After this he hardly bothered to look at anything else. What were roe deer and squirrels compared with wolves? There was only one other place where he constantly turned his gaze and that was where Neska's puppies were. After some thought and exploration he found a spot where he could observe both wolves and dogs with almost equal ease and had the unique experience of comparing their very different and yet parallel existence.

The puppies still mainly relied on the food he brought them but, through the binoculars, Pablo saw how they began to explore and harvest up experiences. Hunger prodded them to fend for themselves. He couldn't bring them enough to satisfy their ever growing appetites without revealing their existence, and he saw how they pounced after birds and vainly tried to catch them on the wing. They were destined to failure most of the time but with greater frequency Pablo saw them chewing at small creatures, perhaps birds or baby squirrels fallen from the trees. It wasn't easy to tell. He never saw them actually catch anything but he knew that they made more and more prolonged forays into their surroundings and usually came back with something with which to while away the hours until he should throw them more food.

They no longer looked for him and even when they saw him, as they often did, they no longer tried to play with him. The male puppy looked at him in a way he found difficult to understand that was not exactly defiant, not exactly trusting, not exactly fearful. His eyes healed and were as sharp as usual but he never forgot the experience and kept his distance from Pablo ever afterwards. The bitch puppy copied her companion in everything. Her nature was far gentler than his but she was correspondingly more timid. Pablo would have liked to play with them, to crush them against him as he had so often done with Neska, but he kept his feelings very strictly under control because any kind of sentiment could only be harmful to them.

In order to protect both himself and them from any weakness, he preferred to watch them from a distance through the field-glasses and, when he discovered the wolves, could hardly bear to abandon the forest at all, completely unaware of time until the failing light made it impossible for him to see.

He learned to tell the difference between the male and female wolf. The male was larger and slightly darker. If they hunted together he usually went slightly ahead, but more often than not one stayed behind to look after the cubs, at least while they were small. They seemed to take it in turns to stay at home and both were equally long-suffering. There were three cubs, looking so much like Neska's two puppies that Pablo wondered what difference there could be between them. They had the same sharp muzzles and pointed ears, the same desire to gambol and growl and sleep in the sun, and to swallow everything that came within

their reach. They still sucked at their mother but with ever lessening frequency. She wouldn't even lay down for them eventually and they had to get what they could in a standing position, usually on two legs, stubbornly clinging on even when she tried to run away from them. In the last of their suckling days, most of what they managed to get was stolen in snatches, when the she-wolf was distracted.

Pablo never spoke to anyone about the wolves, any more than he did about the puppies. He knew that the only way to keep a secret was by sharing it with nobody, not even the person you most trusted, and although he talked a lot to Don Elicio about his observations in the forest, and asked him endless questions which resulted in the teacher lending him his book on Spanish fauna, he avoided any hint of his discovery.

It was a very expensive book, full of photos in colour as well as columns of information. It wasn't easy for Pablo to read because it had been written for adults with very technical words and a lot of Latin phrases, which he skipped because they weren't important. Grandfather made him cover it with newspaper to keep it clean and he told everyone in the bar one Sunday morning how Don Elicio had lent it to him because he knew Pablo could be trusted. All the boys wanted to borrow his binoculars – they thought of all sorts of ways they could use them for fun – but Pablo would lend them to nobody and never took them into the village. They were the key to a private, undreamed-of world, and too precious to be let out of his sight.

The cubs and the puppies were about the same age and they grew at the same rate. If anything, the wolf cubs were chubbier. They got more to eat than the puppies and, as they grew older, they began to follow their parents on their expeditions, learning to hunt mice and insects for themselves.

The puppies managed to catch a rabbit – a youngster that had wandered too far from its burrow and realized it too late. They caught it between them, zigzagging across the glade in which they had found it, missing it several times until more by luck than judgement the bitch puppy grabbed hold of its scut. They made a messy job of killing it; it got away three times but hadn't the strength to travel very far; but Pablo was pleased to discover not much later that the wolf cubs had hardly greater skill with their first hare, which they pursued across the stony ground out in the open and would have lost if the father wolf hadn't turned it in their direction again. Both cubs and puppies had a lot to learn.

Summer came. Pablo passed his exams at school and then he helped Grandfather gather the corncobs from the maize field beyond the orchard. At the edge of this field was a little stone house where the maize was stored. This little house was built on stilts to keep off both rats and damp and there was a stone cross at the highest point at each end. The corncobs were winter fodder for the cows and oxen.

There was a lot of work in the summer with haymaking and harvesting. Everyone had to help. Pablo's father decided it was best for his family to spend the summer at the farm. He had a few days' holiday from the factory and helped with the harvesting. The sun shone down every day and Grandmother brought food out to the fields for them all. She carried the baby on her hip and left her to crawl about over the grass while they washed down the bread and pie with Grandfather's special cider. They gave her chunks of bread to suck and Pablo played with her, tickling her bare toes to make her laugh. She turned bright red in the sunshine and her hair was like fine gold.

At the end of the day Pablo was often too tired to go up to the forest. He leaned with his father against the trunk of an apple tree and showed him Don Elicio's book. Before his father went back to work they went into the forest together. Pablo didn't take him to his special place, from which both the puppies and the wolves could be seen, but they were able to see the timid roe-deers nibbling their way across a glade surrounded by oak and chestnut trees, the calves now almost as tall as their mothers.

Pablo knew that when the summer ended he would have to go back to the city with his parents. They had a place for him at school in September, a school with a uniform, which made it seem very special. Don Elicio told Pablo he could keep the book as a going-away present. He almost blurted out his secret at that but checked himself just in time.

Grandfather measured him against the barn door again. He had grown tremendously and was still taller than his own father at the same age. He remembered being measured the previous summer and looked for the mark that Grandfather had made for Neska at his insistence. So many things had happened since then that surely it wasn't only a year ago! Had Neska shared only a tenth of his life? It had seemed much more than that.

He was to go back to the city with his mother and Yolanda a week before school started, which would give him time to get his uniform prepared and buy the necessary books. There was both excitement and dread at the thought, overwhelmed by regret for the forest he was going to miss. At first it had been only Neska's puppies that had drawn him to its depths, and then the wolves, but now he knew that it was all the forest, with its myriad of trees of every kind, its wilderness of flowers and ferns and fungus-covered dampness which sheltered so many creatures of which he had been unaware until so recently, living out their lives in accordance with the laws of nature while, hardly any distance away, there were people living in accordance with the laws of man.

His parents promised to let him spend the winter holiday with his grandparents and with this he had to be content. He could do no more for Neska's puppies. It was up to them now to survive as best they could within the forest's laws. He had seen enough now to understand that if they were tough and quick-witted they could survive. At least they had been given a fair chance, as he had promised himself for them. It was all that any free animal could expect. It was up to them now to make the most of their freedom. He wouldn't see them again until winter. It was hard to say goodbye, but he was learning.

The whole family spent Christmas Eve and Christmas Day at the farmhouse. The grandparents couldn't leave the animals to go to the city so Pablo's parents spent the night with them. Grandmother was full of both laughter and tears. When Pablo asked her why she cried she said it was because she was happy to have him back with her again. After lunch on Christmas Day Pablo's parents went back to the city. They had chains on the wheels of the car because the road was icy.

The days went by and Pablo didn't go into the forest. He wondered about the puppies, which must have grown almost to full size by now if they had survived, but he was reluctant to look for them. He preferred to imagine them being there, living out there lives among the rocks and trees, the same as the wolves. If he went and didn't find them he would always be wondering what had happened to them. He found enough to do, making friends with the two piglets that had recently been bought and hammering some rails to make a pen for the calves that Grandfather had decided to buy for fattening. He went with him to buy them at a village market a few miles away. They rode on the oxcart and on the way back Pablo sat in the straw with the calves, which were only a few days old, keeping them calm and letting them suck his fingers and knees and jersey.

On the last day Grandmother complained that he had spent most of his time with Grandfather and wanted him to promise to be back for Easter.

'Easter's a long way off,' argued Grandfather, not wanting her to get set on the thing so soon. 'He's got to think about his school work now and not go worrying about us.'

So Pablo went back to his other world, his world of school, football and friendships, all so far removed from the farm and the forest that these didn't even seem real to him when he was away from them.

20

It was some time in January when the first short article appeared in the local newspaper about damage being done in the region by wolves. The article didn't say very much, only that several farmers had complained about losses of livestock and that three different people claimed to have seen wolves at a distance. Pablo never read the newspapers and wouldn't have known about this particular article except that one day, bringing home some potatoes his mother had sent him to buy, his attention was caught by the word 'Wolves' in bold letters on the newspaper they were wrapped in.

When he got home he tipped the potatoes into their box and spread out the sheet of newspaper. It was already several days old. Two villages were mentioned which were in the next valley to Grandfather's.

For the next few days he glanced through the local paper which his father brought home each evening but saw no further news. Time went by and he forgot. In February there was another short article about the wolves. Pablo had given up reading the paper by then and it was his father who saw it and read it out loud one evening. It really said no more than the previous one.

'I wouldn't have thought there were any wolves left in these parts,' he commented. 'It's years since anyone has spoken of them.'

'What about the ones who attacked the village the other Christmas?' Pablo found himself obliged to remind him. 'Do you think they might be the same ones?'

'Who knows? It's possible. I only hope they keep away

from your grandfather's farm this year.'

'If you go there this Easter you'd better keep out of the forest,' warned Pablo's mother. 'It would be terrible if anything happened to you there.'

'Wolves don't attack people,' Pablo retorted.

'That's what you think. They're altogether wicked animals. Do you think people would speak so badly of them if it wasn't true?'

'It doesn't say that in Don Elicio's book. It says – '

'Never mind what the book says. If you think you're going to be wandering about in the forest again like you were last year, I'll not let you go.'

'I expect they'll have been caught by then,' interrupted Pablo's father, sensing the sudden antagonism between the two. 'I expect it'll all be forgotten by the time Easter comes.'

Pablo would have liked to know more about the wolves. He read the article again and again as if by rereading it he would discover something new. He read the pages about wolves in Don Elicio's book again but that didn't help him either. There was also a chapter about wild dogs, cimarrones they were called, which were far more dangerous and destructive than wolves, being at the same time far more numerous. They were found mostly in central and southern Spain but they could also be found in the north. Pablo remembered how Don Elicio had said that most people couldn't tell a wolf from a dog. He thought of the puppies and the cubs and knew he was right.

He thought of the wolves he had seen in the hills and wondered if they were responsible for the ravages being mentioned in the newspapers. He hoped not because he felt a fondness for the wolf family that only he had known about. He wondered about Neska's puppies, which by now must be as big as any wolf, but he refused to admit, even to himself, that either his wolves or his puppies could be responsible. After all, there had been the attack only the winter before in his own village. It didn't let the wolves out, but it did exclude the puppies. And if there were wolves on his side of the valley, surely there could be others in the next valley, too. They didn't have to be his wolves, or even his dogs, and he longed for Easter to come, sure that he would be able to discover the truth for himself.

At last the holiday arrived and once again Pablo found himself on the road back to his grandparents' farm. He had the book and the binoculars with him in spite of his mother's alarm. She had tried to make him promise that he would keep away from the forest but, with his father's assistance, the most that he would promise was that he would be very careful and not do anything dangerous. There had been one more mention of wolves in the press, less alarming because it reported only that farmers were trying to claim from the local authorities for losses caused by predators, so that Pablo's mother couldn't really base her fears on facts and had to be satisfied with his promise.

As usual, Grandmother had been cooking since early morning and they all ate far too much, including little Yolanda who was now toddling round the big living room by herself for the first time. Pablo took her to the barn to see the winter calves which were now twice as big. She didn't like the smell of them and screamed until he took her away. She liked the rabbits better and Pablo caught a baby one for her to stroke. He hurriedly took it away from her when she began to pull its hair. She screamed when he picked her up to carry her back upstairs because she wanted to go everywhere by herself.

While the women were downstairs washing the dishes, the men started talking about the wolves. Pablo listened with avid interest. Grandfather said that no one on that side of the valley had been affected at all. Whether this was because everyone had taken extra precautions to keep the stock locked up, he couldn't say. He had heard only rumours and had seen what the newspapers reported.

'Do you really believe there are wolves in the forest?' his son asked him.

Grandfather shrugged. 'How should I know? Pablo probably knows more about it than I do. After all, he used to spend hours there. Didn't you?' he said, turning to him.

Pablo nodded.

'And did you ever see any wolves?' his father asked.

He shook his head.

'Last year we had a lot of foxes. Perhaps foxes are doing the damage,' put in Grandfather.

'But surely people couldn't mistake a fox for a wolf!'

'People are capable of anything, especially when talking to a newspaper reporter.'

They agreed that it wasn't really dangerous for Pablo to go into the forest as long as he didn't go too far, and as long as Pablo agreed to keep an eye out for any sign of the wolves and to tell Grandfather if he saw them. Both women needed convincing of their decision. Neither of them could see any reason for him wanting to go there. If he wanted to know about animals he had Don Elicio's book and the programmes on television. It looked as though he wanted to worry them on purpose. But the two men defended Pablo and in the end they gave up the argument.

The next day, Pablo pulled his boots on over his jeans and wore a thick jacket with a scarf. It was cold enough for Grandmother to insist on the scarf. She had wanted to wrap it round his ears as she used to do when he was smaller but he resisted that. She made him stuff some bread and cheese into one of his pockets, at the same time telling him to come home for lunch, and filled his ears with warnings and complaints.

Pablo had no particular plan when he set out, except to make for his favourite look-out place. The going was difficult. The meadows were flooded with yesterday's rain and tried to suck off his boots at every stride. The grass was coming up strong. Soon Grandfather would be letting out the calves for the first time, if only he could be sure they would be safe. He suddenly remembered how he had crossed these fields with Neska, so many times.

By the time he had reached his destination some of the clouds had dispersed. Sunshine was beginning to touch the wet trunks and leaves and bracken. The sodden earth was full of jumbled tracks, rabbits, deer, birds, criss-crossing each other, most of them indistinguishable. He looked carefully for paw-marks but saw none. He hadn't really expected to find them so was neither disappointed nor relieved. When he reached his look-out he took off his scarf and jacket and, not without a sense of anticipation, lifted the binoculars to his eyes.

He had already lost the patience he had developed the previous summer and moved them sharply from place to place, aware of nothing but rocks and branches and rotting thickets. Half a dozen times he just missed a squirrel's leap, a roe-deer's tail-switching bound, the flight of a bird, but as he got back into the feel of it his patience and skill returned.

He trained his gaze on the place where the wolves had been. There was still snow in large patches, caught in over-shadowed crevices, lying among the boulders. Slowly, gradually, he brought his gaze over a wider, lower area, feeling his heart beat with anticipation as he recalled how he had so unexpectedly seen them for the first time. Surely this was how it would happen again! But it didn't. Time went by and he saw nothing out of the ordinary. He wasn't sure whether he should be relieved or sorry.

Then he looked for the dogs, training the binoculars on their old place, but not finding them there. While his gaze travelled in a circle, he wondered what had become of them. Had they died? If he looked carefully, would he find their skeletons somewhere among the bracken? Had they eaten poisoned meat in their hunger, and had the crows cleaned their bones as they would have done with Neska if he'd let them?

He looked at his watch, a present from his parents that Christmas. He just had time to go up to Neska's old hiding-place. Perhaps if he looked closely he would find some clue which would answer his questions.

He spent more than an hour searching amid bracken and bushes, turning over stones, digging with a stick among old leaves. He used the field-glasses again and again but found absolutely nothing. All he could be sure of was that they hadn't died anywhere nearby. It was still possible that they were alive.

As he returned to the farm he wondered about those predators in the next valley. How far away was it across the hills? He would ask Grandfather. Even as he thought this he changed his mind. If Grandfather thought he was looking for the wolves he might not let him go. He would find out himself by going there, through the forest if possible, just as the wolves or dogs would go.

The weather favoured his expedition. The next morning, after helping Grandfather with the animals and coaxing

Grandmother into letting him stay away from home longer, he set off at a trot towards the next valley, not wanting to waste any time. From the farmhouse, it didn't seem so far away, but in the forest itself it was difficult to judge distances and not always possible to follow the shortest route. He had to make detours round impassable bracken and thorn bushes, he had to climb rocks and sometimes retrace his steps, and still he was in the same valley with only his own village and local farms in sight. He began to think it would have been quicker to go by road, or even to have followed the river, but he plodded determinedly on until at last appetite gave him an excuse for resting.

It was while he was eating his hunk of bread and cheese that he got the feeling he was being watched. There was a slight rustle in some bushes to his right, which could have been caused by birds, but he could see nothing and it didn't worry him. When he finished the food he used the binoculars again, examining the terrain on every side. The feeling that something or someone was watching him grew and now it began to disturb him, making a prickly feeling down his back. As nonchalantly as possible, he let go of the binoculars and looked more closely at his immediate surroundings.

He was in an open part, on a rocky slope with the nearest trees about twenty feet away, amid a tangle of blackberry bushes. There wasn't a sound except for that occasional movement. Until he listened, he hadn't realized how silent it was. He wondered if it was the silence that gave him the sensation of being the centre of attention. He suddenly realized that his heart was beating as if he had been running hard and he was cross with himself. What was he scared of, after all? He'd been in the forest so many times and he'd never felt scared before. But he had never had this sensation before, either, crawling up and down his back. He wished he hadn't come so far. He didn't know what to do.

Should he stay where he was? If he decided to run, where should he run to? Was he really being watched? He reached for some stones. The feel of them pressed into his palms was comforting and he took the binoculars from round his neck and wrapped the strap round his hand. He could use them to defend himself if he was attacked. They were pretty heavy.

Then, even as he scoffed at his own fears and precautions, the dogs appeared. The bushes which had screened them were pushed aside as they declared their presence, three of them, shoulder to shoulder, jaws open, tongues lolling, eyes staring straight at him.

For a second Pablo felt dizzy with fear until, with a shock, he recognized the biggest dog as Neska, dark muzzled, brindle grey! It was Neska's son, of course, no ghost but that defiant puppy who had looked so much like her that he had wanted to take him back to the farm. The smaller, reddish animal would be his sister. As for the third, it was grey like the first dog but smaller and less heavily built.

The momentary delight at recognizing the puppies halted Pablo's dizziness but a second later fear flooded back as he realized that the expression in their eyes was far from friendly. They had fixed him with a hunter's stare, coldly measuring the distance between them and him, coolly waiting for him to make the first move, absolutely sure of their victim. He clenched the stones, shivering with fear, feeling absolutely sick with fear. If they attacked they would tear him to pieces on the hillside and no one would probably ever find even the smallest trace of him.

It was no good calling to them. He had fed two of them as puppies but they didn't recognize him. They were dogs but they were savages and had no connection with the kind of dogs he had always known. He might have run, except that fear had fixed him to the spot like a helpless rabbit. Then he remembered some words of Grandfather's from one of his hunting tales.

'If he hadn't run they might not have gone for him. The worst thing you can do if you're cornered is run. Remember they can run faster than you.'

So he mustn't run. Grandfather had said that the best method of defence was attack. He must attack them first and hope that they would run. They were certainly in no hurry to attack him. They just stood stiffly staring, with narrowed eyes. The smallest one had crouched down without taking his gaze off him. Pablo noticed that he had inched forward a few paces.

With the blood pumping so fast in his heart and head Pablo could hardly think, but he counted up what he had in his favour – a few stones, the binoculars and his voice. Perhaps if he shouted at them, perhaps if he ran straight at them swinging the binoculars, they would be too surprised to attack him. He was quite sure that, until now, not a single creature they had set their sights on had ever fought back. They were absolutely certain that they had him.

The trouble was he was too scared. His legs wouldn't work. He felt like surrendering to them there and then, just curling up where he was and letting them do as they wanted with him. To think that he had fed them when they were puppies, kept them alive so that now they should tear him to pieces. Their ingratitude infuriated him. They weren't going to make a fool of him! They were only Neska's puppies, after all, and he had beaten them more than once.

He began to think of all the worst possible insults for them – he had learnt quite a lot at school that year – and once his blood was up he forgot his fear. He threw the stones that burned in his hands with all the force that possessed him, running towards them at full speed, screaming at the top of his voice, swirling the binoculars round his head and bursting into hysterical laughter as he saw how they fled in three different directions, absolutely startled by his unexpected behaviour.

The small grey dog turned round to come back at him and Pablo caught it across the haunches with the binoculars, sending it yelping into the bushes. The female had already disappeared and the only one left was the big male that looked so much like Neska. He had stopped at a distance, panting, eyes narrowed but without that certainty they had expressed before. Pablo rushed towards him, swinging the binoculars again, yelling like a Red Indian. He grabbed up a big stone on the way and flung it with all his might. It didn't hit him but it made him run.

Within seconds the clearing was empty. The dogs had disappeared and Pablo was alone, shaking all over, already wondering if he had dreamt it. Then he was overcome by nausea and his legs doubled under him. He found himself being sick and crying as he had never cried in his life, tears and sobs pouring out of him as he trembled uncontrollably. This fit passed and when he came to himself again he realized he might still be in danger. The best he could do would be to get back home as quickly as possible. He no longer felt the presence of the dogs and was almost sure they had given him up, but even so he still felt terrified as he ran back the way he had come, hardly daring to stop although his lungs were torn with pain and his sides ached.

He stopped when he came to a thicket of thorn bushes under which he crawled, quite sure that even if they were near they couldn't attack him. It was uncomfortable but safe. He stayed there for some time until at last he was breathing and thinking normally again. He realized even more clearly now the terrible danger he had been in and that luck rather than judgement had saved him.

Just thinking made him start shaking again, so he decided to move on, feeling more secure the closer he grew to the part of the forest he knew. Soon he could see his grandparent's farm and felt tears of relief spurt to his eyes. Now he knew he was safe.

21

Pablo said nothing to his grandparents about what had happened. He kept out of their way as much as possible, still feeling traces of the panic that had possessed him in the forest and sure that they would sense it. He didn't feel hungry and went to bed early. Grandmother came to tuck him up. She pressed her hand on his forehead and felt his palms.

'Are you sure you're not feverish?' she worried. 'You look very pale to me.'

'I'm all right. I'm just tired.'

'I expect it's the fresh air. I don't suppose you get as much now as you used to. You'll be getting all that contamination they talk about on the radio. Yes, it's the air that makes you sleepy.'

She kissed him and pulled the blankets up round his ears. Then she went away.

Pablo couldn't sleep. He kept thinking of his encounter with the dogs and every time he remembered the look in their eyes his heart beat fast again. He went back to remembering how small those two puppies had been, how he had first seen them with Neska, how they had followed him, tumbling and playful, refusing to believe that he didn't want them. Their eyes had been bright, full of innocence then, looking to him for all that they needed once Neska had gone. They had been as any other puppies, like Neska herself. He had played with them, held their soft, wriggling bodies in his arms, felt their tongues over his face, their little teeth scratching his fingers, and although he hadn't expected them to remember him, up there in the forest, it was impossible for him to understand how those two little creatures had become ferocious killers.

He could not doubt their ferocity – beads of sweat broke across his forehead as that calculating stare, bereft of any expression but murderous intent, bored yet again through his mind. And that third dog! Perhaps he had taught them to kill, perhaps he was responsible for the blood-thirst that was in them. It occurred to him that this was the animal responsible for Grandmother's slaughtered chickens. Perhaps he had been living in the forest all this while, had come across the pups and taught them all he knew.

He remembered how he had seen the two puppies killing their first rabbit, gambolling with waving tail and bright eyes until, almost by accident, they had pinned it down. They hadn't really needed to hunt seriously for food, still depending on him for their needs. Hunting had been a game. But then he had gone away and hunting had become a necessity, the means to survival.

What had happened in the forest that day hadn't been a game. They had been in deadly earnest, of that he could have no doubt. They had tracked him down as they would have tracked down any other animal and they hadn't really been afraid of him. He had taken them by surprise, that was all. They could just as easily have called his bluff and, had they done so, he wouldn't now be lying in the farmhouse bed with the blankets tucked under his chin.

He tossed and turned in the bed, indignant, afraid, bewildered. That day he had made discoveries beyond his understanding. He had been close to a horrible death; he had stepped beyond the bounds of his everyday life and come up against a harsher way of existence; a way he had observed and read about without really understanding. He had blamed the farmers for Neska's death and it seemed just to him that from time to time the forest animals should steal from them. It was a retribution he could understand. It fitted in with the ideas of right and wrong that he had been taught at home and at school. But there had been no question of right or wrong in what had happened in the forest today.

There had been no more than a primitive instinct for survival.

His mistake had been in believing that because he meant them no harm, because he went only as an observer, they would respect him. He had felt safe in the forest, in spite of other people's doubts, because he had meant no harm to any of its inhabitants. That was how the rabbits and deer lived, harming nothing as they nibbled their way across the glades, and they were the ones that died. Now he understood and was frightened.

At last he drifted into sleep and his dreams were full of Neska, the wolves and the dogs.

The next morning he fed the calves for Grandfather and watched while he milked the cows, wondering all the time whether he should tell him about the dogs or not. It would mean confessing that he had lied before about Neska's puppies, telling him of the deceptions he had practised to keep them alive and, worse still, having to tell him what had happened in the forest the day before. It was all very complicated and he was loath to begin, especially when he thought of the terrible fuss Grandmother would be bound to make.

Yesterday he had been frightened of the dogs. Today he couldn't hate them. He had been indignant because he had fed them when they were small and expected them to be everlastingly grateful. Today he could understand that his thinking was mistaken. They were on the other side of the forest. He had gone into their territory. He had got what he deserved.

No, he wouldn't tell Grandfather. Summer was coming. It would be easier for the dogs to hunt in the hills now. They would stop attacking the farms and perhaps by next winter they would have moved somewhere else. The wolves had already gone.

There was plenty to do on the farm with Grandfather, enough to fill his hours without going to the forest. The farmer wanted to get the calves out to pasture but there was a lot of dead grass which needed tearing out first. He had another field which had been left fallow since autumn which now needed preparation for sowing and it was also time to get the manure out of the barn and onto the land. It was one of his busiest times and most of the work had to be done single-handed.

When the animals were fed he gave Pablo a rake and a shovel and told him to start digging out the old straw and load it onto the oxcart. It was a job that would take two or three days and Pablo's hands were blistered before it was time for lunch. He thought he had worked very hard but when Grandfather came back he said, 'Times are changing. If your father hadn't done more than that at your age I wouldn't have given him his dinner.'

Grandmother overheard and rushed to Pablo's defence. 'He's here for a holiday, not to work. Fancy giving him a job like that anyway! Pablo, you go down to the village this afternoon to play with your friends. You've done enough for one day.'

But Pablo liked the job in spite of the blisters and back-ache. He liked helping Grandfather and the next day he wrapped a couple of rags round his hands to keep them from blistering more. In the afternoon he helped Grandfather in the field. It was very near the forest, with a steep slope. Grandfather went round the fences with a big roll of wire and a heavy mallet. In a lot of places brambles covered the old wire, making it stronger. Pablo held the loose posts still while Grandfather hammered them into the ground and he helped unwind the new wire which was needed in places.

'I don't know why my father works in a factory. When I grow up I'm going to help you on the farm,' he told Grand-father. 'I don't want to stay in the city.'

This was true. He could imagine nothing better than living and working on the little farm, feeling the sun and the rain, preparing the soil and combing out the grass – because the work they were doing in the calves' meadow was like combing a particularly rough and unkempt head of hair. Now and again he gazed up at the forest, which was bright in that afternoon's sunlight, the chestnut trees heavy with white flowers. His fear had gone. The incident with the dogs was like a bad dream which, like all bad dreams, faded with daylight.

Helping Grandfather, the days flew by and soon he was back at school in the city again, struggling with geometry and algebra during the day, fighting for mastery of the football in the afternoons and gently teasing Yolanda at night. His parents and grandparents lived in two different worlds and, although he could find pleasure and occupations in both, the farm and the forest were part of him, the part that moved him most.

There was no more news in the local paper about wolves. They seemed to have been forgotten. Pablo had got into the habit of glancing through the pages, just in case, but the absence of news made him believe that the dogs found enough to eat in the forest without needing to go down to the farms. He was convinced in his own mind that the dogs had been responsible for the various attacks already reported. Surely it was too much of a coincidence for there to be both wolves and dogs attacking villages in the same district at the same time? Anyway, it no longer mattered because the attacks had ceased and not even Grandfather mentioned them when they all went to spend a weekend at the farm.

Pablo spent more than an hour just staring at the calves which were now half-grown, sturdy and plump. He didn't know if they remembered him but they were friendly creatures, overcome by curiosity at the sight of him, unable to stop staring at him until eventually the boldest decided to make a personal investigation. He had brought some bits of cotton cake, broken up in his pocket, as well as the block of minerals that Grandfather had asked him to leave in the field, and they chewed up the cake and licked at the stone and one of them even tried chewing his shirt sleeve. Their noses were black and wet, their eyes soft and limpid, like the eyes of the roe-deer. Flies crawled up and down their faces but they didn't mind.

It was only a few days after this visit that Pablo's father

drew attention to an article in the newspaper that day, only this time it wasn't the local newspaper but a national one. It claimed in letters half an inch high that a pack of wolves was sowing panic in the mountain villages. In one place several pigs had been killed, in another a dog had been eaten. The wolves appeared in broad daylight and were unafraid of humans. A shepherd claimed that a sheep was stolen from his flock under his very eyes, regardless of his efforts to frighten off the predator.

Pablo couldn't believe it. Why should they suddenly start attacking again? Was it really the dogs, or was there also a pack of wolves in the region as the newspaper claimed? How could he possibly know? He wondered about the dog that had been eaten. He supposed the poor thing must have been chained up, unable to defend itself. But would dogs eat one of their own kind? Could they be so hungry or so ferocious? He was horrified.

Perhaps the story wasn't true. Grandfather himself had doubted some of the stories and Pablo knew that, more than once, he had told tall stories himself. But surely the newspaper wouldn't print things unless they were true. He didn't know what to think.

22

Suddenly wolves became news. Hardly a week went by without the national newspapers reporting some episode or another and the local paper went on with its account of angry farmers and the deaths of numerous domestic animals. There were even reports on television and Pablo was surprised one lunchtime to see on the screen a face that he knew. It was Don Elicio who, surrounded by a crowd of farmers and other onlookers, was giving his opinions to a television reporter in the main square of the town where Pablo had bought his bike. This town was central to the villages of the district and it appeared that the local authorities had been besieged by farmers who were unsuccessfully claiming compensation for the animals they had lost.

Don Elicio had been chosen as the spokesman for his village but his personal opinions were not altogether in agreement with those of the local farmers.

'I don't think that wolves are responsible for the damage,' he was saying. 'The villages are full of hungry dogs which often take to the hills and breed there. No one in our village has seen any of these predators close enough to be able to state positively that they are wolves. In fact, I doubt if anyone among us is in a position to be able to make such a claim. None of us are experts and any wolf-dog at a distance could be taken for a wolf.'

'But they ought to pay us,' broke in a farmer, shouldering himself between the teacher and the reporter. 'Wolves or dogs, our stock's being killed or maimed and the authorities are doing nothing about it. The professional hunters pay for a licence to be able to go and shoot wolves in our hills, so there must be wolves there, or where do they get their trophies from? We're not allowed to shoot them without a licence and yet they can come and kill our stock whenever they feel like it!'

'What do you say to that?' the reporter asked Don Elicio, pushing the microphone against his chest.

'I maintain that the wolves stay in the hills, which is where the hunters find them. They don't come down to the villages. They're afraid of man. They keep away from him. They've suffered enough in the past to know that man's a killer.'

'The farmers are saying that the wolves should be exterminated as pests. Do you agree?'

'I appreciate the farmers' feelings but I can't go along with the opinion that every wolf in our forests should be exterminated. In this country we're still lucky enough to have a few wolves and they should be protected by the government. The farmers should be paid compensation but the wolves should be protected.'

'A sum of money doesn't compensate for the work that goes into rearing a good milk-cow,' growled someone behind him. 'Its all right for you, and people like you to talk. You've got nothing to lose.'

The reporter turned to this new voice. 'Do you think wolves are doing the damage?'

'I don't know and I don't care. I say we should organize a full-scale hunt and then we'll find out whether they're wolves or dogs.'

'Do you think the wolves should be exterminated?' the reporter asked someone else who only grinned and shrugged in reply.

'What about you?' He thrust the microphone at a small, wrinkle-faced farmer.

'Yes. We should get rid of them, and as soon as possible.'

'What do you say?' he asked the man next to him, a youth this time.

'I think we should organize a hunt. It's no good waiting for the authorities to do anything. We must do it ourselves.'

The report was interrupted there, much to Pablo's

disappointment. His mother hadn't seen it. She was in the kitchen, washing the dishes and talking to Yolanda who followed her around like a dog. He decided not to tell her about it.

Only a few days later the hunt was organized. At least a hundred men from several villages were taking part, plus several sportsmen who had hunted wolves in different parts of the country. They were interviewed on television and were generally convinced that they would bag at least half a dozen animals. Most of the men were acting as beaters as few of them had licences for rifles sufficiently powerful to kill a wolf, and they went along with pots and cans and clubs, with the hope in their hearts that something would fall into their hands. Boys and dogs went along, too. The television cameras filmed them setting out and promised to give a report on the result in the news that evening. A well-known authority on Spanish wild life gave his opinion that they wouldn't catch any wolves, but the public in general hoped that he was wrong. They didn't like his whitewashing of the wolves' reputation, any more than they liked his criticisms of bull-fights and women who wore fur coats.

Pablo could hardly concentrate on his school-work that afternoon. His mind was in the forest, whose silence was being trampled by excited, angry men, and he hoped that both the wolves and the dogs would escape if they were there, because a hundred men against a few animals seemed most unfair to him. He wondered if Grandfather had joined the hunt. He wondered if Don Elicio had protested. He wished he was there – at the same time glad that he wasn't – and it seemed that the hot afternoon would never end.

The report on television that night was very short. The result, so much anticipated by both farmers and experts, was three wolf cubs, about eight months old and a dog, unlucky enough to have been crossing a field as the hunters went by. No one could really believe that the cubs had been responsible for the attacks. They were far too young, but at least they proved that there had been wolves in the forest because now there were three less. There was an article in the news-

167

paper the next day, together with a photo of three smiling hunters holding the three cubs upside down by their tails, asking whether the hunt should have taken place and whether the cubs should have been shot, but then the whole thing was forgotten. For the moment, both farmers and hunters were satisfied.

Pablo grieved for the cubs. He wondered if they were the offspring of the wolves he had watched all summer and how the adult animals and the dogs had escaped. Had the cubs only fallen because they were young and hadn't learnt to be wily? Would the others be frightened away and leave the farmers in peace?

One result of the television publicity was that Pablo's mother didn't want him to go to the farm that summer, certain that it was dangerous. Some friends had invited them to spend a month by the sea and she wanted Pablo to go with her because he had never seen the sea and the salt air would be good for him.

'The mountain air's good too,' he insisted. 'You've said so yourself and, anyway, I promised Grandfather I'd help him with the hay-making. Papa promised to come, too. Grandfather can't do all the work by himself.'

'He managed in the past. He can do it again.'

'The other farmers helped him before because they knew he didn't have anybody to help. But now he's got me and Papa.'

She didn't have an answer to that and so she said she would think about it. She knew Pablo was determined to go and that he would probably get his own way. Most of all she wanted him to be happy. In the end it was decided that Pablo should go to the farm, joined by his father for the hay-making week who would afterwards spend the second week of his holidays at the sea, taking Pablo with him if he wanted to go.

The first thing Grandfather did when Pablo arrived was take him to the barn door to be measured. He made a new notch with his knife, at least two inches higher than the last one, chuckling delightedly. Grandmother had come to watch the measuring and afterwards they all looked at the different notches, including the fading ones, and talked nostalgically about the years gone by. Grandmother wiped a few tears from her eyes and Grandfather laughed, saying she was getting sentimental in her old age.

They all walked across the meadows to look at the grass which was waiting to be cut. The two men discussed their plans and the weather while Pablo looked up at the forest, its trees all dark with full summer foliage, wondering about the dogs. In the evening they sat in the orchard and sharpened the sickle blades while Grandmother peeled runner beans and potatoes for their supper.

Grandfather had given Pablo a short-handled reaping hook, easier for him to manage than the big ones, and he was practising on the grass in the orchard, feeling a sense of power as he grabbed a handful of grass with his left hand and chopped it through with one stroke of the blade. He was slow at first because his father had warned him to be careful about standing too close to the grass he was cutting. 'You don't want to cut off your legs, too,' he told him, but as the evening wore on he worked himself into a steady rhythm, lost in the pleasure of it and the smell of the grass in his nose.

How his back ached when he stood up, hearing Grandmother calling him for supper! He could hardly straighten it. They all laughed at him but after supper Grandmother brought him some liniment made with rosemary which his father rubbed into his back before he went to bed. They shared the same big bed that night, which pleased Pablo tremendously, and talked for a long time before going to sleep.

The next day they began cutting the grass, Pablo round the edges with his small reaping hook, the men working their way slowly up and down the sloping meadow, leaving the fallen grass in wide strips behind them. When they all stopped for a drink of cider Grandfather said it was a perfect day for hay-making, with the sun bright but not too hot and a breeze blowing in their direction to keep them fresh.

Grandmother had gone down to the village for some groceries but not before she had put a sheet of meat pasties in the oven for their lunch which she would bring to the meadow when she came back.

But when she did reach the field she wasn't carrying the expected basket. Her face was flushed with hurrying and she waved her arms and called shrilly to her husband and son who were in the highest part of the field. Pablo reached her first.

'What's the matter?' he cried, noticing how upset she was.

'Something terrible's happened. Something terrible.'

She waited for the others to approach and then she gave them the news she had heard in the village. It concerned Santiago's family.

One of his sisters had been playing outside the house that morning, the new house which Pablo had helped to build, when a wolf appeared and tried to carry her off. Her screams brought everyone running to the scene and the wolf escaped in the chaos. Her parents had rushed her to the hospital at the doctor's advice – some of the bites were severe and she would have to be treated against a possible rabies infection, too – and all the family and most of the neighbours were so incensed that they had sworn to burn the wolves out of the forest. From what she had been able to gather, they had already gone up there to set all the undergrowth on fire.

'They're mad!' exclaimed Pablo's father. 'With the dry weather we've been having they'll start something they won't be able to see the end of.'

They all looked towards the trees. Santiago's farm was just over the hill. If the flames really caught, if they didn't have the sense to think twice, the chances were that the breeze would blow it towards them.

'I'll get over there and find out what they're doing,' said Pablo's father.

'Can I go with you?' cried the boy.

'No. You'd better stay here. Keep a watch on the trees from this side and if you see any signs of the fire run down to the village and get as much help as you can. We must just hope that not everybody will be trying to promote a fire. There might be a few people left who'll help us to put it out.'

Pablo went back to the farmhouse with his grandparents. They had a much better general view of the forest from there and so they sat outside, eating their pies and watching the trees. Pablo didn't feel hungry. For once Grandmother's delicious pastry stuck dryly to his tongue. The memory of his experience with the dogs had come back to him with full force and it was as if he could feel their soulless stare on him again.

He thought of Santiago's little sister and couldn't understand why the dog – or wolf – had attacked her. There were cattle in the fields, chickens in the yard, pigs rooting in some of the oak-treed pastures. Had it chosen the little girl as the easiest, most helpless victim of them all?

'What's the matter, Pablo?' asked Grandmother, noticing the food still uneaten on his plate.

He shook his head. 'Nothing. I'm just not hungry.'

How could he tell them now that he had known about the dogs all along, that he, in a way, was responsible for what had happened today? Oh, how he hated those dogs now, hated them for their insatiable cruelty. And to think that they were Neska's puppies! He felt like crying, afraid of what he had done, or of what he had neglected to do, but he was more afraid still of confessing what he knew. He blinked a few tears from his eyes and tried to swallow the pie that was stuck in his throat.

'I expect you've been working him too hard,' Grandmother complained to her husband, taking the plate from Pablo's hands .'You'd better lie down for a while,' she coaxed the boy. 'And don't worry about anything. Everything will sort itself out. I don't suppose the fire will get very far.'

He allowed himself to be led up to bed, comforted by Grandmother's assertions, and very soon fell asleep.

23

Grandmother was wrong about the fire. Even while Pablo slept the first clouds of smoke began to float over the trees and slivers of flame began to catch in the undergrowth. There had been no rain in the district for more than a fortnight. The sun was hot and much of the bracken was hollow and dry.

Hardly an hour after the raging men had thrown down their first lighted matches, they were hurriedly hacking at branches with which to beat back the uncontrollable flames. More and more people joined them, Pablo's father among them, battling furiously to halt what had been so recklessly begun. Several hours later they were too exhausted to continue. Two men had collapsed, most of them had burns on their hands and arms, and hardly any of them could either breathe or see in the thickening smoke. It was becoming too dangerous to stay on the mountain, with the breeze chasing flames in every direction, and they had to leave it to the experts.

All that night the fire ate up the forest. Pablo watched it, down in the orchard with the rest of his family. Grandfather had brought all the stock down to the next field and the animals were restless at the nearness of danger, stamping, snorting and lowing for most of the night.

Nobody said very much, too affected by the glow which lit up the whole valley. Sparks flew up whenever a giant tree crumbled. Now and again whole sheets of flame brightened the reddened sky. It was the most impressive thing Pablo had ever seen.

He thought of all the small animals whose homes were in those trees. What would become of them? Would some of them escape or would they all perish in the flames? And even if some survived, where would they make a new home? What would they eat? And what of the dogs? Would they perish, too? He hoped so with all his heart. It wouldn't be fair if they escaped while the squirrels roasted in their nests and the rabbits suffocated in their burrows.

At last Pablo was sent to bed. His father and Grandfather decided to have a look at the highest meadows to make sure that none of the fences had caught fire but they wouldn't let him go with them in case there was any danger.

By the time he awoke the next morning the fire had been extinguished. A plane from the forest fire service circled above the still smoking hillsides for most of the morning but at midday it disappeared. The breeze that was usually so welcome on a hot day brought only the acrid reminder of destruction and Pablo looked at the forest with sadness in his heart. He had nothing with which to compare that desolate aspect; stark, blackened trunks, many of them completely branchless, protruding with harsh nakedness from the scorched ground where smoke still spiralled. Even in winter he had never seen the forest so bare and unprotected and the trees which had escaped the flames, looking doubly green that morning, only intensified the black and grey colours of the lifeless. The carbonized trunks made Pablo think of a jungle of blackened bones, twisted fingers stretching in agony towards the sky, and when e saw them like this he was too frightened to go on looking.

They were able to continue with the hay-making that morning although the grass smelled of smoke and there was a film of ash on every blade. Grandfather hoped that as the grass dried out and was turned before being collected the smell would disappear. Pablo worked furiously, afraid to lift his head and see the suffering forest – for he knew inside himself that it was suffering – but in spite of this he couldn't rid his mind of the image that had come to him that morning.

In the night he dreamed of the three dogs. They were big and black, with reddened eyes. None of them looked like Neska. They looked like phantoms, solid of body and yet unreal, running through the naked, smouldering trees whose trunks were crusted with thick black scabs. He could hear and feel the breath which panted from their jaws, rhythmic, unhurried, terrifying just because it was so unhurried. They knew. They were sure of themselves. Then he felt his own breath which was stopped in his throat and bursting in his lungs.

He was running through the forest too, much faster than the dogs, but although he knew he was running faster, twisting and turning through the trees, they were gaining on him. Each time he looked round they were nearer, and yet he knew it couldn't be so. He sped along with heart-stopping panic, sometimes brushing against the trees. His hands were black. Everything was black: trees, dogs, earth, hands, sky.

And now they were on him! The biggest dog leapt straight at his back. He couldn't see it but he could feel the leap with all intensity and screamed. His father's arm, falling across his shoulders, woke him.

He sat up in bed, his heart beating as if it would burst, his mind struggling with dreams and reality. His father woke up at the same instant and asked him what was wrong but at that moment he had no voice and couldn't answer.

'You're dreaming,' he heard him say. 'Come on. Lie down. Get back to sleep. Don't be afraid. I'm here with you.'

'The dogs . . .' He shuddered involuntarily.

'There aren't any dogs. Get back to sleep,' he coaxed him. 'It was just a bad dream.'

He gently pushed Pablo down, who still resisted, and pulled the bedclothes over his shoulders. Within a minute his unhurried, regular breathing told Pablo he had fallen asleep again. Pablo's heart, which had calmed down slightly, began to beat fast again because the sound reminded him of the dogs in his dream. He knew now it was a dream but the panic he had felt stayed with him. He fought against closing his eyes, sure that once he did so he would be back in the burnt-out forest, pursued by the dogs who wanted to kill him because only he knew of their existence. They wanted to get him before he told anyone, before he sent anyone to hunt them down and kill them.

His mind wandered to Santiago's little sister, playing in the yard outside the house, not much bigger than Yolanda, and he imagined the biggest dog, the one that looked most like Neska, watching her, gradually inching forward, patient though rapacious, judging the best moment for the attack . . . .

He jerked himself awake, feeling sleep treacherously overcoming him, and this time his willful mind went back to that day when he was alone on the hillside and the dogs had followed him.

He was scared of sleeping but he was so tired. His head felt so heavy and his eyes wouldn't stay open. He wouldn't think of the dogs. He would make himself think of other things, nice things, such as . . . He grasped wildly for something nice. The calves, for example. They were sweet, gentle creatures with soft eyes and wet muzzles, but then he saw the dogs creeping down the pasture to the unsuspecting, tail-swishing little group, and again a feeling of horror overcame him. Tears slid down his cheeks, tears of defeat. He just couldn't escape them no matter how . . .

He jerked himself into wakefulness again to find the morning sun filling his room with floating specks. His father had already gone without waking him. Normally he would have dashed out of bed, not wanting to miss a minute of the day, but this morning he felt tired and defeated, still affected by the nightmare which had almost immediately returned to his memory.

Should he tell everybody about the dogs? Would it make any difference now? Surely they had been destroyed in the forest fire. But supposing they hadn't? Wouldn't they come again and again, attacking people, perhaps attacking Grandfather's calves? They had been clever enough to escape the hunters before, clever enough to escape poisoned bait and even the traps he had heard his grandfather talking about. Perhaps they had escaped the fire, too. Not all the forest was burnt, after all.

He tried to imagine himself confessing. Everybody would blame him for what had happened to Santiago's sister. Suppose it had been a wolf and not one of the dogs? After all, he couldn't be a hundred per cent sure that both dogs and wolves were not responsible for all that had been happening lately. Perhaps he was blaming the dogs unfairly. . . . But the memory of that day at Easter forced him to be honest with himself. He knew it was the dogs. No one else really knew, and it was his duty to confess. It would be terribly hard but he would have to do it.

He couldn't imagine what Grandfather would say. Perhaps Grandmother would defend him. He felt sure that he could make Grandfather understand. He knew how much he had loved Neska and how impossible it would have been for him to let the puppies be destroyed too. He felt he could make him understand, if not at first then eventually. But his father . . . He wasn't often stern but there were times when Pablo was almost afraid of him and those times had been for lesser faults than this. No, he couldn't tell his father. He would be shocked and would never understand. He would wait until his father went away. He would be going very soon now. Then he would also have a chance to find out if the dogs had been destroyed in the fire. Someone might know something, some news might be brought. In fact, it might not be necessary to say anything at all.

On reaching this conclusion, Pablo felt strong enough to get out of bed. It was late. Grandmother had left everything tidy in her little kitchen but was nowhere about. Perhaps she had gone to the village. He helped himself to a mugful of milk and cut a hunk of bread from one of the loaves in the larder cupboard. He didn't bother about washing as there was no one around to make him and, still chewing the bread, made his way to the second meadow, for they had finished the first the night before. He had forgotten his sickle and had to go back for it and both his father and grandfather laughed at him and called him a sleepy head.

The next few days were peaceful enough. They finished the mowing and, with the sun both constant and brilliant and not a cloud in the sky, they were able to rake up the drying grass fairly quickly, leaving it in small stooks because it was still a bit damp. Grandfather said it could set on fire by itself if they didn't give it sufficient time to dry out. They must just pray for the good weather to continue before getting it into the barn. For that job the two oxen were yoked to the wagon and Pablo set the stooks in layers as they were thrown up to him. By then his father had gone, knowing that Pablo and Grandfather could finish the job by themselves and that his wife was growing impatient at the seaside without him. She had sent them a postcard with a view of the beach, saying that Yolanda just loved the sea water and begging Pablo to join them.

When the postcard arrived, he had considered leaving with his father. It had come the same day that he had decided he might have to tell Grandfather the truth. Here was a chance to escape and he almost jumped at it. Then he saw that Grandmother looked sad – she couldn't help not wanting them to leave her so soon – and he said nothing. Grandmother had brought the postcard from the village. She told them that the cause of the fire was being investigated and that things looked difficult for Santiago's family.

'Poor things! As if they haven't enough to worry about with that child of theirs still in the hospital. Enough to frighten her to death, such an experience, let alone all the pain. It's a wonder she survived.'

This reminded Pablo of his duty so that when his father actually asked him whether he was going to leave with him or not, he could only answer that he wanted to stay, although he still didn't know if he would have the courage to confess.

There was no news of either dogs or wolves.

24

Days went by. It was very hot and as there was so little for the village children to do Don Elicio organized some swimming lessons at a place on the river beyond the village which was safe for bathing. Pablo enjoyed himself so much that he was always sorry when it was time to go home. By the end of the week he could swim about ten strokes, which was as much as Santiago could do. Then it rained for a couple of days and no one went to the river.

Pablo felt very restless. From the upstairs window he watched the rain pour down over the blackened forest, wondering if there was still life under the frizzled bracken, and if the rain would give it hope. The field-glasses were in his room and, giving in to temptation, he went to get them. Afterwards he wished he hadn't. It was bad enough seeing the destruction from a distance. The strong lenses made the details far too vivid. He could see the carbonized branches almost under his nose.

There were no birds or squirrels, or anything else that he could make out, and this reminded him that he still hadn't told Grandfather about the dogs. Perhaps it wouldn't be necessary now. As far as he knew there had been no more talk about wolves. Either they had gone somewhere else or had died in the flames. He certainly didn't want to have to confess and, as each day went by with the same tranquillity, he pushed the idea further and further from his mind. In a month's time he would be back in the city. He decided that, if nothing else happened in that time, he would keep quiet.

It was surprising how quickly the time passed. Don Elicio went away on holiday but his pupils promised to practise swimming although he wasn't there to guide them. One day when Pablo came to the bank he found it deserted. He went on to the village to buy himself some chewing gum at the baker's, who told him that the evening before a group of boys had discovered three wolf cubs in an abandoned cottage not very far from where they had been playing and swimming all this time. His heart almost stopped beating at the news.

'What have they done with them?' he asked the baker.

'As far as I know, the father of the boy who found them has still got them. I don't know what he intends to do with them. Drown them, I expect.'

The news of the wolf cubs was all over the village and the parents of the children who had been playing by the river all these days were absolutely horrified to think that they might have been in terrible danger. Had the cubs not been found, no one would have imagined that wolves would dare to bring up their young so close to human habitations. It just went to show how daring they had become, attacking in broad daylight, trying to carry off a child and now even giving birth to their young in a ruined house hardly more than a mile from the village.

Pablo discovered that the farmer who had the cubs was at the bar, talking about them to whoever wanted to listen. This was most of the village so he hurried along there, too.

'What are you going to do with them?' was the question everyone was asking.

'Do with them?' He stared round at his audience, men, women, children, all equally fascinated, and couldn't help feeling important. 'Do with them?' he said again, savouring the moment.

Pablo's heart beat wildly. If he was going to kill them it would be his fault for not confessing about the dogs. Perhaps there was still time. If he told everybody now about the dogs they would know it hadn't been the wolves. But even as this thought flashed through his head he knew it would make no difference. He couldn't imagine him letting the cubs go free. How he wished he could see them!

'Where's he got them?' he whispered to a boy standing next to him.

'In his barn, I think, in a box.'

This was enough for Pablo. He didn't wait to hear what the farmer had planned to do with them. His longing to see them was far too strong. He knew where the man's barn was, about a quarter of a mile from the village, and he ran all the way there. There was no idea in his head beyond that of seeing them, no feeling in his heart other than indignation and fear for them. He would have to do something to save them.

The barn door was shut but it wasn't locked. Pablo looked about carefully but there was no one in sight. He lifted the wooden latch and opened the door a few inches, just enough to squeeze himself inside. A rustle of straw, a ferocious growl, and a dirty white mastiff flung itself towards him, checked suddenly by a chain which nearly dragged it off its feet. Pablo had stiffened with fright at the first movement and, even though the dog couldn't reach him, he trembled all over. The dog barked madly, eyes threatening what the chain prevented, and Pablo was torn between the desire to flee and the desire to go over to the big crate which he had noticed in a corner and which must contain the cubs.

At that moment the door was flung wide open and a stout woman appeared. She looked at Pablo suspiciously.

'What are you doing here? What do you want? Who gave you permission? You want to think yourself lucky that the dog was tied up. He could have torn you to pieces. What do you want? Come on. Speak up.'

She didn't give him a chance to, snapping, 'What's your name?' as he opened his mouth.

'They told me the cubs were in here. I only wanted to look at them. I wasn't going to do anything else.'

'You keep away from them. They're dangerous.'

'Can't I just see them?' he begged, emboldened because she now looked at him less harshly.

'You're the boy whose parents are from Germany, aren't you?' she said, ignoring his question.

He nodded, wondering what that might have to do with it.

'Well, you can have just a quick look. But don't get near them, mind. They might be small but they're as wicked as the very devil. Shut up,' she shouted at the dog, which began barking again just as soon as Pablo moved.

She took him over to the crate, picking up a stick on the way. Through the slats Pablo could just make out a jumble of grey furry bodies, flattened together as closely as possible in one corner. Three pairs of eyes stared back at him, sharp with terror. The woman pushed the stick through the slats and poked at the cubs. By their reaction they were used to being poked. They attacked the stick with growls and snaps, at the same time trying to shrink away from it.

'See,' said the woman with satisfaction. 'Put a finger in there and you'll get it bitten off. Now be off with you and don't let me see you in here again. The dog might not be tied up the next time and I'll not be responsible for you.'

She pushed him to the door when she saw that he lingered and stood in front of the barn, legs apart, hands on hips, watching his progress down the road. He looked back twice, so he knew. She didn't trust him and wouldn't move from there till he had gone.

He returned home, filled with misery. He didn't want to go back to the bar and listen to the farmer, certain that he was going to kill them, and his momentary wild hope of being able to rescue them had been dashed by the woman and her dog. Poor little cubs. They could hardly be more than three or four weeks old. How frightened they must be, imprisoned in that dirty crate, poked with sticks and probably very hungry. He remembered the cubs he had seen on the mountain, just like the puppies, gay and playful, harmless looking. They were probably harmless, too, but even the most harmless creature has to defend itself. How would that fat woman like to be poked and looked at? Wouldn't she fight back?

He couldn't understand why the parent wolves had abandoned the forest to have their cubs in such a place. Was it true, after all then, that the wolves had been responsible for all the recent attacks, living so close to the village, while he had been blaming the dogs all this time? His mind struggled to understand. He had been so certain about the dogs, so certain of the wolves' innocence.

As he plodded homewards he lifted his eyes and saw the forest before him. Each time he looked, it still gave him a shock because he never remembered it except as it always used to be. A month had passed but still he expected to find the forest as green as always. He imagined the wolves being burned out of their haunts, fleeing before the ever greedier and greedier flames, obliged eventually to take shelter in the valley, instinctively seeking the river.

Of course! That was the reason. How could they live in the forest if the men had burnt them out of it. They had to live somewhere else and the mother wolf, heavy with cubs, desperate to find shelter for them, had given birth in that ruined cottage as the only safe place, near to her enemies though it was. The cubs were too small to be more than a few weeks old. Surely they must have been born at about the time of the fire, perhaps the very same night. It must have been very soon afterwards for, if not, surely the wolves would have found a safer, more distant place than that.

Where did they go to hunt, he wondered? There had been no more attacks in nearby villages. He remembered from Don Elicio's book that wolves were capable of travelling a hundred kilometres in a single night. They must have been away hunting in the unharmed part of the forest when the cubs had been found.

How could he save them? How could he save them? He asked himself that question again and again, coming up with no answer. He wished Don Elicio hadn't gone away. Surely he would have spoken for the cubs. He would have thought of some way of saving them.

What about the wolves when they came back? Would they know before they reached the ruins that the cubs had been stolen from them? Would they sense what had happened there? Again Pablo's heart began to beat wildly as he realized that he had been so busy thinking of the cubs' fate that he hadn't thought of their parents'. Everything was suddenly clear to him. They would use the cubs as a bait to catch the wolves. They would set a trap, an ambush, into which the anxious parents would surely fall. That was why they hadn't already killed the cubs. First of all they would use them to kill their parents.

Pablo felt as though his heart and head would burst. It was all the fault of the dogs, all his fault for having kept silent about them. The farm animals, Santiago's sister, and now the wolves and their cubs, all sacrificed to those wild dogs he had fostered in the forest. There must be some way of preventing it. Surely he could save them if only he could make everyone believe that the dogs had done all these things and not the wolves.

They wouldn't listen to him, perhaps, but if Grandfather told them, surely they would take notice. They knew Grandfather wouldn't lie to them. He had no cause to. He was just as anxious as everyone else to rid the district of the killers. If he could make them all believe that the killers had been Neska's puppies, gone wild in the hills, surely everything would be all right. They couldn't kill the wolves then, just for the sake of killing them. Some of the farmers might think like that but not all of them. If only Don Elicio were there! He would defend them.

With these thoughts, just one fervent hope, he rushed back to the farm.

25

'Pablo, what's the matter? What's happened?' cried Grandmother, frightened by the strained look on his face as he appeared in the kitchen doorway.

'Where's Grandfather? I've got to talk to him. It's terribly important. He's got to come down to the village with me. He's got to help me.'

'I think he's up in the top field, mending a fence or something. But stop for a minute, Pablo. Tell me about it first.'

But he had already gone from the doorway, running, stumbling, almost dizzy with anxiety and lack of breath. Grandmother hurried after him but she couldn't catch up with him.

Pablo poured out his tale just as soon as he reached Grandfather, rubbing the sweat out of his eyes as he spoke, completely unaware of the state he was in, hardly even aware of how he told the story, knowing only that time was against him, that Grandfather must help him, that he must know everything at once. Grandfather was still on one knee, giving a last twist to a bit of wire, when Pablo began to shout out his confession, and he listened with bewildered amazement, trying to stop the boy with questions which Pablo didn't even hear.

Once Pablo cried impatiently, 'Listen, Grandfather, you've got to listen to me. You've got to do something,' and then he rushed on. By the time he'd finished the farmer wasn't quite sure if he really knew what Pablo was talking about.

One thing he did gather, when at last he stopped talking, was that somehow or another he was expected to save the

wolves and that the look in his grandson's eyes told him
that he believed him capable of it. By this time Grandmother
had reached them and she was already cross because she was
out of breath and frightened by Pablo's behaviour.

'Really, really!' she began. 'What a way to come home!
Frightening me to death – '

'Now don't you start,' interrupted her husband. 'The boy's
very upset and your grumbling isn't going to help him.'

He put his arm round Pablo's shoulders. 'Let's go through
this again calmly,' he suggested. 'Then perhaps I'll know
what you want me to do.'

'I want you to save them,' he cried impatiently. 'You can
if you want to. I know you can.'

'Ssh!' Grandfather put up his hand. 'I don't know what
I can do until I really understand what it's all about.'

'But I've told you. Neska's puppies and – '

'You've told me a long, complicated story which doesn't
make much sense. I want to sort it out for myself and I want
you to answer my questions. Honestly, too. No more lies,
because I gather you've told me a number of lies in the past.'

Pablo hung his head. 'I'm sorry, Grandfather. If I'd known
what was going to happen . . .'

'It's too late to be sorry. Now let's go through the story
again.'

As they did so, Pablo had a feeling that Grandfather
wasn't going to help him, even before he actually said so.
He couldn't make him understand why he had lied about
the puppies and Grandmother exclaimed angrily when he
admitted how he had stolen food for them and spent so
many hours in the forest for their sake. He had expected
them to be angry but he had thought that their anger wouldn't
matter as long as they did something. He hadn't thought how
hurt they would be by his deception.

At last Grandfather said, with a gravity in his voice that
Pablo had never heard before, 'I think you yourself realize
now what a bad thing you did when you lied to me. You're
responsible for all the terrible things that have happened.'

'Don't say that to him!' protested Grandmother with

tears in her eyes. 'How can you say such a thing?'

'Because it's true!' His voice rose to a shout. 'Our neighbours and other farmers have lost animals, money and time. That little girl might have been killed. Pablo himself . . . and all for a stupid sentiment about a couple of puppies.'

'He didn't understand,' excused Grandmother. 'He's only a child.'

'I told him the puppies couldn't stay in the forest. I told him at the time, didn't I, Pablo?' he demanded, turning to him.

Pablo nodded weakly, unable to look up, struggling to understand himself why at the time it had seemed right to do it when now it seemed so wrong.

'And you lied to me. You told me they were dead.' His voice was a harsh accusation.

'Because they killed Neska,' he shouted back. 'They had no right to. You yourself said so. They deserved to lose something, too.'

'Would you still think like that if they'd killed my calves, the calves you helped me rear this Christmas? Can you still think like that after what happened to Santiago's sister?'

'But I didn't know,' he moaned. 'I never thought . . .'

'That's why you should have listened to me. Do you think I enjoy drowning puppies? Eh?' he demanded.

Pablo shook his head.

'Then if I do it it's because I have to. Because there's a reason for it. I thought I'd made you understand that at the time.'

'It's your fault too,' declared Grandmother, anxious to protect Pablo in spite of everything. 'You shouldn't have believed him, knowing how upset he was about Neska. You should have gone up there yourself, to make sure. Ah, Pablo, Pablo!' she sighed with all her heart. 'Why ever did you do such a thing?'

'I didn't think it would matter. I was going to tell you, Grandfather,' he cried, looking up at him earnestly, 'but then – '

'But you didn't, and these things were happening and all

the time you knew about the dogs and said nothing! I just don't understand, Pablo. I wouldn't have thought you capable of so much deception.'

'He didn't realize,' Grandmother answered for him, hugging him close to her, unable to resist the tears that were welling in his eyes.

'Perhaps he didn't, and I don't think you realize what might happen if this story gets about the village. People will blame me for all this. Who knows if they might not make me responsible for all the damage? I might even have to pay the hospital bill for that child.'

'Do you think that's possible!' she exclaimed.

'Why not? Everyone's furious, as you well know. If they're mad enough to set the forest on fire, they're mad enough to come after me for their money. And I'd like to know where we'd be then.'

'But if no one knows about it,' said Grandmother, hoping to calm him. She turned to Pablo anxiously. 'Pablo, have you told anyone? Have you said anything at all about this to any of your friends?'

He shook his head, trying to blink back his tears.

'Are you sure? You're not lying again, are you?' demanded Grandfather.

'Don Elicio . . .'

'What about him? Have you told him?'

'No. I promise I haven't. Only, it was Don Elicio who made me think Neska might have puppies in the forest that time I couldn't find her. It was his idea.'

'But did you talk about it to him afterwards?'

Again Pablo shook his head. 'I didn't say anything to anyone,' he insisted. 'It was a secret.'

'Thank goodness for that at any rate!' Grandfather seemed slightly relieved in spite of his anger.

Pablo took advantage of the moment to put in consolingly, 'Anyway, Grandfather, I'm sure the dogs must be dead. They must have died in the fire. There haven't been any more attacks since then, have there?'

'Perhaps you're right, or perhaps they've escaped to the

other side of the hills. Only time will tell. Meanwhile you're to say nothing about this to anyone. I'll go and look for them. There might be some traces.'

He looked at Pablo severely and took hold of his chin.

'I know you didn't want to harm anyone,' he said. 'I know you felt very badly about Neska, but you have to understand that life is like that. Keeping those puppies alive didn't help Neska. It didn't help anyone. It only did lots of harm. Dogs aren't wild animals and when they run wild they're worse than all the animals in the forest.'

'I didn't know.'

'But if I'd told you that then, when Neska died, you wouldn't have believed me. You would still have lied to me, wouldn't you? You would have thought you could change things because you didn't like them the way they were.'

Miserably Pablo looked at him. 'And the wolves?' he asked.

Grandfather sighed and dropped his hand. 'You'll have to have them on your conscience, too,' he said. 'I can't possibly tell the people in the village what you've told me.'

'You won't do anything?'

'What can I do, Pablo? Do you want to ruin me?'

'Won't you even go and see what you can do?' he begged.

He shook his head. 'I'll look for the dogs, but that's all I'll do, and now you'd better get back to the house and clean yourself up. I don't want you to go down to the village again until all this business is over. Do you understand?'

'But, Grandfather – '

'You heard what I said.'

'Yes, but – '

'Come on, Pablo,' broke in Grandmother. 'Don't upset your grandfather any further.' She pulled at his arm coaxingly.

He went back to the farmhouse with her, unable to believe that Grandfather would do nothing, unable to accept that things could be so wrong and yet not be put right. He had no appetite for the food Grandmother piled on his plate, trying to comfort him, and went to lie on his bed, wondering in the semi-darkened room why things should turn out the way they had.

He thought of Neska and her puppies and the days he had spent in the forest observing both the dogs and the wolves. He felt sure that the cubs he had seen then had been the ones that had died in the hunt. Now, if they trapped the parent wolves too, that would be the end of them on that side of the forest. Like the eagles Grandfather had spoken of, they would be no more than a memory for some, while most people wouldn't even care. He had wanted to give new life to the forest and had only succeeded in causing destruction. He had wanted to do good and great harm had come of it. He couldn't really understand why but felt too defeated to cry.

Grandfather wouldn't let him go down to the village for several days and those days he spent in silent agony, wondering about the wolves. He dared not even ask and no one spoke about them although both knew that he was suffering for them. The farmer spent hours in the forest daily, coming back with an acrid smell in his clothes. He took his gun with him but had no cause to use it. There weren't even any rabbits or wood pigeons. Only time would tell what had become of the dogs.

One day, after he had been in the village, he called Pablo to him and told him what had happened to the wolves.

They had tied the cubs to a stake in the centre of an open space in front of the barn, with the barn door open and the the light glowing out in the darkness. The cubs had begun to whimper, obviously aware that the parent animals were not far away, and the wolves had called to them. The first night nothing happened but on the second they were obviously unable to resist the call of their younglings. With tremendous caution both animals stepped within the circle of light and were shot just as soon as they did so. With some ten rifles waiting for them, including those of the local Civil Guard, they hadn't a chance of escape.

The cubs were being kept in the barn, still, and the farmer who had them treated them well enough. He fed them with milk and bits of meat and the authorities talked about arranging for them to be sent to a zoo.

'I don't think anyone wants to kill them,' he said, 'so you can stop worrying about them.'

'They might as well be dead as be in a zoo,' protested Pablo miserably. 'They belong to the forest.'

Grandfather sighed. 'The truth is, Pablo, they belong to another time. You wouldn't find a single person around here who would defend your point of view.'

'Don Elicio.'

'Perhaps, but he doesn't have to earn a living from the land.'

Don Elicio came back only a few days later. He was very interested in the cubs and shared Pablo's feelings about sending them to a zoo. He asked Pablo if he wanted to see them but, although his heart jumped at the words at first, he shook his head. He needed time to forget and seeing those cubs wouldn't help him. He had lost his war and knew too that his cause had been a mistaken one. He would leave this new cause in Don Elicio's hands, knowing that he cared.

Don Elicio worked hard. After a number of visits to different authorities, with form-filling and letter writing and telephone calls – all grown-up things which Pablo would have known nothing about – he managed to make arrangements for the cubs to be taken to a national game reserve, where they would be released in the forest just as soon as they were considered capable of taking care of themselves. It was more than Pablo could have hoped for, after having given up all hope – a place for them to live in freedom, protected by the law.

When his parents came with Yolanda to take him back to the city, he wasn't sorry to go. It had been a hard summer one way and another but in spite of that he knew he wanted to come back. The snow would be covering the forest in only a few months' time and under the snow the ground would keep warm and fertile. By spring, perhaps, new leaves would be flowering. It would take years for the forest to recover altogether but at least by spring that recovery would have already started and he wanted to be there to see it.